UNEARtHLY

Find out what makes some of our smallest fears turn into nightmares in this treasure trove of short stories.

Sometimes it feels like we are all on a different planet earth.

Sometimes we are.

Manufactured in the United States of America
Designed by Magic Pen Designs

CONTENTS

UNEARtHLY

When Calian the Ansect had finished being downloaded into his new Husk, his first feeling was of anticlimax.

This is the animal that so many of my brothers refuse to exploit? He thought, looking down at the weak, fleshy digits of its hands; and the bent, aching feel of its skeletal structure. *I wonder why even the high queens avoid them, for this does not seem a savage planet.*

Calian had taken Husks on many more dangerous worlds; the soft, pink, and pitiful form he now inhabited seemed less than threatening.

Humans, he thought, flexing his pallid hands before his weak, unimpressive eyes. *Feeding here will be plentiful.*

He was impatient for the download to finish so he could begin his hunt.

"Before this Husk expired, it was called Allen Cummings," a digital voice interrupted, prolonging his impatience. "Now that you are restoring enough necessary functions for life, it will receive your assigned name, Calian Carter." Calian was an imperfect translation of his Ansect name, made pronounceable by the primitive vocal cords of his new Husk. Carter was, of course, simply human gibberish, allocated to give order to their obviously disorganized world. He accepted this bit of information without resentment and waited for his transfer into the Husk to be complete. Normally, it did not take this long. He felt the organs of his new body shifting, rearranging, and responding to the energy beaming down from the Hive. Needless to say, this did not hurt, as translation into a husk never hurt; however, new Ansects could find it mildly curious.

This Husk must have expired violently, he thought, for even though the membrane of his skin was healed.

He noticed blotches the color of rust covering the floor, and walls of the tiny room in which he found himself. Oxygenated blood was not uncommon on many of the planets where Calian had ventured, and he was therefore familiar with it. The shifting of his organs slowed, and the slight hum that had filled his senses vanished. At last, the translation was complete. Calian took a step forward. His human Husk was surprisingly sturdy, given its number of limbs. He longed to try them out in running and jumping – those things which every Ansect relished in the hunt.

On most planets, newly awakened Ansects found themselves out in the open when their translation was complete, their Husk bodies ready to burst into fight or flight. Not so with the humans, apparently. Rather than awakening in one of the many jungles or plains the human's planet had, Calian was discontented to discover that he was enclosed in a dim, gray room that was nearly uniform on all sides. Behind him there was a series of paddings piled on each other, obviously used for reclining this inefficient human body. They were the color of dead moons. Artificial sources of light waited in several corners, as, Calian was unsurprised to find out, human eyes were weak in darkness.

Then I shall hunt in the dark, he thought.

Even in a Husk, an Ansect had other senses on which to rely. Calian heard a rustling, then a thumping. Startled, and noticing with grim satisfaction that a 'heart' organ was now pounding in his chest; hearts, in general, made for easier targets. He approached the edges of his uniform confines and placed an ear against it. The sound of breathing, matching his own, and raised voices. Knowledge of his Husk's language had been included in the download, but these voices were too muffled to make out clearly. Still, there were other humans! Prey, an arm's length away! Excited, he crossed the room, and placed his ear against the opposite barrier, a "wall" the translation in his head provided, and he smiled as he recognized the herding sound of even more humans. Tens, hundreds, maybe even thousands, all contained within this uniform block!

At this knowledge, a familiar but terrible hunger awoke in Calian's stomach, and he felt, without meaning too, some of his natural Ansect weapons bursting from his Husk's skin. Claws, teeth, serrated carapace flesh, all the natural hunting weapons that could be infused in a waiting Husk, accumulated over the galaxies and millennia...

Then, Calian noticed again the strange red stains that coated the wall of his room in all directions, which caused him to wonder just how the previous Husk had expired, sending its old Ansect spiraling back into the Hive for reassembly.

Perhaps hunting in these cell blocks will draw attention to myself, he realized.

Through a transparent pane of glass in one of the walls, he saw there were more humans down below, all milling and ambling completely unprotected. Calian felt his stomach growl at the sight of them.

So much easy prey, he thought. *But how to get to them?*

At first glance, there was no obvious way out of the grey cube in which he found himself. Some things he could recognize the uses of, like the primitive, black computer machine that sat on a wooden block, or "table", his translation provided, in the corner. There was a door, but he knew, after he glanced out, that it lead merely into the innards of the grey cell building, and he quailed at the thought of becoming lost in that featureless, engine-room maze. It was through the window that he could see his prey, so it was through the window he would go. He approached it, saw that its maker had cleverly designed it to slide, and opened it. The climb was not far – what humans would call "five stories" – and his hunger gave him strength, as well as the claws to grip the crumbling, modified stone that armored this building. He knew he was being wasteful, for extending the Husk body beyond its natural state was calorically demanding. However, at the same time the smell of fresh humans so close by reassured him. The planet's sun had fallen, so no one saw him scuttling down the outside of the rectangular building; nor heard the shower of debris he left as his black nails dug holdings in the brick.

The natural light had been dimming when Calian started his translation, but now it was fully dark, and the number of humans, to his regret, had diminished with it.

That doesn't have to be a bad thing, he thought. *It is always good to hunt the first prey of its kind alone.*

Calian did not suspect any sudden impressive physical manifestations from these humans, but nonetheless it helped him to be cautious. Therefore, when he spied a narrow crevice between structures – what humans would call an "alley" – he was quick to dart inside. Maybe he had invested time studying the flora, and fauna of this planet – which many Ansects did before entering a husk – then he would have known his movements were spider-like, twitchy, and abrupt; naturally making his prey more wary of him. Calian had not studied, for he had hunted on many planets, and he was confident of his success.

After all, hunger is the most powerful driving force in the living universe, he often told himself.

Eventually, he spotted a loner. A female, adorned in a flickering fabric that did little for warmth, and nothing in terms of armament. Calian attributed this to yet another strange habit of the humans. Even her feet were artificially warped and twisted to resemble- for reasons he could not fathom- what looked like Ansect feet, rather than the flat, wide-spread human's.

She'll be slower with those modifications, he realized. *Good.*

He picked up his pace, careful to hide his fingertips beneath the fabric hanging that had come with the husk; as they were still bristling with black, chitin- like nails. The girl noticed him, and she too sped up. Calian smiled as he felt his Husk's 'heart' organ thundering with the thrill of the hunt. They turned a sharp corner into another darkened alleyway, and with no exit in sight, the female froze. She was stuck in hesitation as she sought in the gloom for somewhere to go. Calian was so delighted to have his prey already cornered, he barely noticed in time that they were not alone.

"Hey, sweetcakes, whatchoo doing on the streets at night all alone?" A deep, drawling voice asked. To Calian, the guttural display of aggression sounded primitive and silly, but he could not deny that the hackles of his Husk went up.

Turns out, there *was* another exit to this alleyway, but it was hidden in the deep by coolly, sweating shadows. From the dark, three young males emerged. Calian could not see their sex, but he could tell they were male by the slung-shoulder swagger with which they approached, and the distinctly masculine scent of domination. Calian scowled as he did not want his hunt frustrated by these lowly meat bags.

"Go away," he croaked, trying out his voice for the first time. It was harsh, and almost painful to use; he found it to be a disgustingly coarse method of communicating. All in all, he judged it useless, for as he repeated his command all that happened was that one of the males barked, "Fuck off, faggot." Then, they ignored him.

"Please, Malcolm, leave me in peace," the female said. Calian was astonished at how different her voice sounded from his, and the intruding male. It had a fluttery lightness to it, like a piece of fabric caught in the wind. In this moment, fear made her vocals high, and soft.

"I told you not to come round these parts," the leading male – Malcolm, the female had called him – growled.

"This is my home!" The female shrilled, "I'm not leaving it for the likes of you!" Calian heard defiance in her voice and was puzzled by it. Why would a weaker specimen attempt to deny the stronger? It was pointless and self-defeating. Every Ansect knew this.

"Then you shouldn't have testified, bitch," Malcolm hissed. The female winced at his menace, but retorted, "they threatened Lydia! You know what she means to me, and…" She trailed off, for something had caught her eye, and strangled the protest in her throat. It was Malcolm, stepping forward while drawing something from a fold of his clothing: a long, thin, silver blade. For a moment, Calian was astounded. Was this male another Ansect in a Husk, armed with a different sort of downloadable violence? He realized, rather quickly, that this was not the case. The blade was a singular object, not an extension of his flesh, as it would have been if we were a Husk. Just a human weapon, threatening another human with its violence.

Perhaps these are his hunting territories, and she has invaded them, Calian surmised. The group of males that clustered around Malcolm did have the look of a pack to them. *Either way, this is good for me. Let the humans weaken each other, and then I will go in for the kill.*

Malcolm lunged, the other two males fanning out on either side of him. The female screamed and pressed herself back against the alley wall. Her breasts rose in terrified gasps, and Calian could tell there was much good meat in them. The two side males pinned her there. Their biceps swelled with muscles, and Calian realized there was enough meat here for a feast.

And why don't more Ansects hunt here? He thought yet again.

Meanwhile, Malcolm stepped back, and pocketed his knife. By the moist crackling of his throat, Calian guessed he was laughing. He watched as the male reached down to pluck at the binding of his clothing, right at the fork of his legs. Calian did not know why he was doing this. Perhaps there was another weapon hidden there? Regardless, he knew enough about hunting to realize that none of them were paying attention to him.

This, he thought, *is the time to act.*

He freed his hands from his clothes, to unsheathe his claws like Malcolm had unsheathed the blade. Except he had long, thin, black, deadly points of death bursting from the tips of his fleshy pink fingers like a separate creature emerging from what gave his human body its name: *Husk.* Calian knew little of Earth's wildlife, but there was a type that every Ansect had heard of, for it was one that reminded them greatly of themselves:

Cordyceps, a type of fungus that infiltrated the body of an insect, and then, in an explosion of growth, emerged from the mutilated husk of the dead insect. Calian knew- with his claws splitting open the skin of his fingers, his jaw detaching as well as elongating, and teeth like mandibles erupting from his fleshy pink lips- that this was exactly what he looked like. No one saw him because everyone was looking at the girl, and she was staring in horror at Malcolm. Calian lunged! He aimed for Malcolm's hand, the one that had wielded the weapon. His claws closed around the forearm, and the skin fell away like cheese forced through a grater.

"Argh!" Malcolm bellowed in horror, wrenching his hand from Calian. This only made things worse, for his flesh stuck to the barbs of

Calian's claws and continued to peel away until a glimmer of bones was visible. Later, Calian would learn the human word for such an injury is 'degloved.' It was a word that would make his stomach rumble with hunger even while grinning with delight.

Blood spurted everywhere. The other males saw the extent of the wound, turned the color of exposed bone, and ran down the alleyway out of sight, and without another word. The female remained pressed against the wall, as if the males were still pinning her there. Her eyes darting from Malcolm to Calian, and back again; they were blank, and glazed, as she was without understanding. Most people when seeing the flesh from their elbow to the fingernails torn away like a chicken wing sucked clean, would have screamed, fainted, begged, or bargained. But Malcolm was tough for a human being, and he balled up his left, uninjured hand into a first, and swung it as hard as he could at Calian. Calian, with unearthly reflexes, decided not to dodge the blow, but to bring his mouthparts to it.

The skin on Malcolm's knuckles vanished as if Calian had chopped it away with a cleaver. Yet another delightful human word! This time Malcolm screamed, and ran.

Calian glanced at the female. She was still pressed against the wall, unmoving except for the rapid fluttering of her chest. He thought about switching his attention to her, but he had already tasted Malcolm's blood. Once he tasted an animal's blood, he would stop at nothing to consume it. So, he chased the injured male down. Malcolm was fast, so Calian was forced to call on even more of his power to catch him, elongating his silly human feet into padded soles, and talons. The demand made his insides bawl, and clamor with hunger pains; but Calian ignored it. He knew he would be eating soon. Malcolm made it about a quarter of a mile before finally turning to face Calian, knowing that he'd lost. In spite himself, Calian was impressed with this endurance. Especially when considering the amount of vital fluids the male had lost.

Perhaps humans are not so weak, after all, he thought.

But then he reached forward, and Malcolm screamed; his long, barbed claws penetrated the human's flesh as easily as roasted meat, with juices spurting all the way to Calian's chest. Malcolm's shrieks turned high pitched, like a whistling, and then Calian thought...

Perhaps not.

It took three large bites for him to die, and every gulp was, to Calian, delicious.

****

After the extensive meal, Calian ambled back to his cell room – or "apartment", as he suddenly realized it was called- even though the sun was rising, he was not in a rush, and spent the journey back licking the blood, and viscera from his fingers. His claws had long since faded, returning him to the Husk's normal state, but there were still some juicy bits clinging beneath the fingernails. Though he was full, he did check to see if the female was still present on his way back. To his disappointment, she was gone.

Once the apartment building came into sight, Calian realized he was beginning to feel lethargic. Normally, after a big meal, many Ansects would enter a digestive state which they would call a *torpor*. They remained aware, of course, but their actions slowed down, and they felt the need to rest. Calian was familiar with the symptoms of *torpor*. It normally befell him once he had returned to the safety of his nest/hole/shell/pod/crater/apartment/wherever his Husk would naturally retreat to. It wasn't so much an exhaustion, as he knew other predatory species often experienced- with more a deep contentment with the world- a happiness to simply sit and digest one's fill. What Calian was experiencing right now was nothing like that. His feet dragged, his brow felt heavy, and his eyes ached to focus. He considered harnessing his Ansect abilities, but in the end decided against it. What if he came out of the transformation and was even more afflicted? With his moist human eyes dry, and itching, Calian finally reached his apartment complex. His mind had finally filtered enough to inform him that there were stairs available, as opposed to climbing up the face of the building. When he entered to look for them, he noticed an invention that was instantly familiar:

His Husk mind told him it was an elevator, but it reminded Calian forcefully of the sliding tube methods of moving deep within the Hive. Suddenly, Calian felt a great nostalgia for his home, which surprised him, because he had never felt such a thing before. He suspected that if it wasn't for his Husk mind, he would not have recognized the emotion. He deduced the etiquette of the elevator immediately, pressed the button, and entered. It was all he could do not to collapse to the floor then and there. The elevator was comfortable to the Ansect mind- small and compact- but he knew it would be strange to be found that way. He had also slurped up as much as the visible blood as he could, but he could not guarantee his cleanliness. Certain species were particular about that, and he imagined humans were among them.

At last, he reached the appropriate level, and stumbled out of the elevator right into another female waiting to board.

"Drunk," she scoffed, and Calian considered eating her, and then decided it wasn't worth the energy.

He dragged himself to his door, forced it open, and fled inside. As soon as it clicked shut behind him, he fell to his knees.

What's going on with me? he thought, as he felt his consciousness spinning.

There was a strange weightlessness to his thoughts, and yet his body felt immensely heavy, so much so that he could imagine the skin sliding down off his bones into a gelatinous pool at his feet.

This isn't torpor! He panicked. *What's going on?*

His Husk mind came in answer, a very human word: 'Sleep.'

Sleep? Sleep? he thought. *That evolutionary dead end that afflicts the weaker species?* Even if humans needed sleep, why would he? Husks were nothing more than vessels, and he shouldn't have to worry about silly animal maladaptation while possessing one. He had experienced this with none of the other hundreds of species he had inhabited for the hunt.

Strange species...strange planet...

His thoughts seemed muddled and slow, not at all like the streaming, chilled clarity he was used to.

What was the male's name? He mused distantly. *Malcolm?*

He tried to recall everything he could about Malcolm, hoping that it might give him a clue to warding off this terrible sickness. It was strange, then, that the last animal he pictured before finally drifted off was not the male's face, but the female's.

****

Calian dreamed. That was a word that did exist in the Ansect vocabulary, though it was used quite differently from how humans used it. To Calian, a dream was a passive state in which he received orders, thoughts, and impressions from a high queen. In this trance, he and all his hunting brothers were united, and harmonized. It was a sort of dissolution of their individual consciousnesses, which was essential to preserving the hive mind that started their whole civilization. This meant when Calian dreamed, he was never alone.

Until now. Perhaps alone was the wrong word. There were a million images: faces, screams, slaps, caresses. They all plagued him while he slept, as he had no shield for them. He was alone amid the swarm. Malcolm's was the face he saw most often. At first, he could not tell it was Malcolm, because the face that swam into his view was so different from the one he'd encountered in the alleyway. It was small, delicate – *young,* his Husk mind realized, no more than a boy – without the lines of anger and hatred which formed around his eyes. Calian did not know how he knew those lines were from those things, but he knew it as certainly as he knew that Malcolm was male, and the creature he had been attacking in the alley was female. It was inherent human knowledge, filtered to him through his husk.

Young Malcolm's face was wet with tears. He clutched at a ragged teddy bear while two large humans, towering over him, argued and fought. As young Malcolm and Calian watched, the larger of the two – the male – reached out and swiped at the face of the smaller one, who was female. By Ansect standards, it was a feeble blow, without claws or weapons, but the female human, Mama! The word suddenly burst into Calian's mind as she screamed and clutched at her jaw. Blood dribbled from her lip, but strangely, Calian felt no appetite. The large male stormed off, and young Malcolm toddled on puny legs towards the woman with his arms outstretched and seeking. The woman ignored him, and instead fished a bottle of amber liquid from behind the couch, from which she began to drink. The smell of it was harsh, bitter, and reminded Calian of the Hive. The dream shifted. Malcolm's boy-face aged, until he looked like a slenderer, softer version of the Malcolm Calian had met. The same large male was back.

Funny, thought Calian, *that I do not think of him as father, even though the biological evidence is there.*

The height difference between the two had lessened, and Malcolm's voice had deepened, coarsened, and roughened, so now when they shouted it seemed like a mirror image attacking itself. The mother sobbed in the corner, forgotten, while the two men came to blows. The old man chipped Malcolm's jaw, while Malcolm split his ear. There was a final cry of anguish, and Malcolm left the house, his mother's sob for help snapped off as abruptly as the slamming of a door. Older now. Malcolm's face had hair on it, and though his skin was dark, his knuckles were white with scar tissue. Him and another pack of men swarmed around two females, cheering at their nakedness, and laughing at their fear…

He had hardened wrinkles, but not yet that evil look. In Malcolm's hand was a bouquet of flowers, and we were walking up the front porch of that house he'd fled so long ago. His muscles were hard and strong, but there was sorrow in his heart, and his feet shifted nervously before ringing the bell. But he was not alone. Men in blue, armed with steel weapons that Calian had never seen but which Malcolm recognized as deadly. They stormed into the house, and their steel weapons exploded with a terrible thunder. The man fell, and then the woman, and all the while Malcolm screamed, the flowers dashed to nothingness upon the porch's wooden floor…

Calian awoke with a start, then turned to vomit all over the apartment floor.

****

When the blackened, chunky gorge on the floor had finally dried, and Calian felt well enough to stand, his hunger returned; more powerful and terrible than ever before. Pangs like animal paws clawed at his insides, and every time he breathed his throat seemed to rattle with emptiness.

Malcolm was not enough, he thought. *I need more of this human flesh to satiate me. But whom?*

This thought had never occurred to him before. On other hunts, he would go for the weakest prey when hungry, or the strongest when he was looking for a fight, and yet, either way, convenience ruled. But now…he sensed that, deep down, where his digestive juices rumbled, and the savage beast of his hunger scraped and gnawed, there were humans who *deserved* it more. But who? His mind did not hesitate before providing an answer. He remembered them from his dream, dressed in blue and smug in their violence. *Police officers.* And even as he voiced the thought, he could hear a rumble of laughter coming from the depths of his throat. It sounded different from his original speaking voice. Deeper. Angrier. Like Malcolm's when he mocked the girl in the alleyway.

The throat must be hoarse from sickness, he told himself, and thought little more of it.

A blue-dressed man would be a challenge, he knew, and though he was sick, he knew he would relish it. He waited until dusk, spending most of the time dozing with his hands clamped over his stomach in pain. At last, the sun of this planet fell, and he arose. The anger in his gut told him that he could find blue-garbed men in the clubbing district. He followed a visceral compass until he found himself at the top of a block of lights, shadows, screams, and laughter. All thronging with sinking bodies, steaming with sweat that made his mouth water in anticipation. In the alley beside him, he noticed a drunkard. So inebriated that he could barely light a cigarette, let alone rise to his feet to run. Calian knew that he would be easy prey, but he ignored him. There was too much anger throbbing in his gut, which the useless vagrant would not satisfy. He made his way forward, at first made anxious by the crowd, but also grateful for its camouflage. In another setting, he would appear grimy and covered in sickness; but here, he fit right in. This made him angrier.

Stupid, weak, disgusting humans, he thought over, and over.

Eyeing their shrieking nonchalance with distaste as they stumbled out of doorways, exposing the meat of their flesh carelessly to the night air. Their smell was so rank that it made him dizzy, hungry, and nauseous all at once. Forcing him to wonder if he would have the strength to make his kill. Then he saw a blue-dressed man, and all thoughts of fear and hesitation evaporated, steamed into nothingness by the heat in his gut. A roaring filled his ears, like water hissing over hot metal, and already he felt the Ansect part of him responding to the hunt. His jaw lengthened, his teeth sharpened, and black spears began emerging from his fingertips. He fought it. The blue-garbed men were dangerous, and he needed to get closer before he attacked. He could see that there was one, leaning against a brightly painted car, and that he had the metal tube on his waist that instincts told Calian meant death. He would need to be close enough to spring before he could draw that tube. Fortunately, a crowd milled about him, brushing close, yet leaving him isolated like water parting around a stone in a river.

He approached with the long black garb of his coat hung low, hiding the talons already springing from his feet. He kept his fists clenched to keep his claws from sprouting and had to wipe the dribble from the sides of his mouth with the back of his wrists. The officer either did not see him or did not care that he was there. For he was too busy lolling against the car, his feet splayed in masculine aggression, a smug grin of superiority lighting up his features as much as the flashing, colored lights of his car. The sight of that stupid smile filled Calian with rage, and though his will thundered against it, he felt his own claws drawing blood from the tips of his hands as they fought to emerge.

The officer's arms were folded, far away from the gun. Calian was merely feet away now, and the stupid man was not even looking at him; too busy winking and whistling at fleshy females as they waddled by. This only served to feed Calian's rage, which had spread from his stomach up to his heart and down to his groin. It was painful in its strength, almost as bad as hunger.

Almost.

Nearby, a group a young people staggered out of a barroom door, tripping over a cement ashtray, and slamming spectacularly onto the concrete below. however, they seemed unhurt, and clumsily helped each other up, laughing and joking when they did. Several of them fell again in the effort, and giggled harder. Calian heard the officer speak.

"Fucking losers," he muttered under his breath. "Asshole's ruining everyone else's good time."

He put his hand to the metal tube on his belt and stepped towards the tittering cluster. Calian did not know what it was – his flinty, poisonous words, the look of violent joy as he approached the harmless group, or just happenstance – but suddenly, he could control his rage no longer. It burst forth like a shattered dam, like a levee overflowed, and like the thunderous flood of a hurricane, he swept for the officer. His lower jaw unhinged, swinging free like the mouth of a snake about to engulf its vermin. His feet turned into talons, and his legs grew stronger, piling up their power before releasing into a mighty leap at the man. If Calian had been thinking clearly, he would have gone for the hands, or the weaponized tube itself, but his rage was overpowering. Instead of disarming or pinning the man, he attacked in a way which made his anger seethe. That stupid mouth, and those stupid fucking grinning lips.

His jaws closed over the officer's face, lacerating the skin in an instant and sending spurts of blood gushing down Calian's throat making his stomach roar so loud it filled his ears, and blotted out his senses. He chewed as the man shrieked, and his flesh tore further until Calian felt his fangs bumping against the flat, and useless surface of the man's teeth. Calian smiled, thinking of how weak and pointless the man was. Distantly, he heard the passerby screaming, and the sound of pounding feet, and Calian chuckled as he imagined the sight of the pair of them – a black toothed monster consuming the face of the officer. He looked like a demon, taking and kissing the man in a hellish embrace. It did not occur to Calian that there were no words for "demon" or "hell" in his language, or in any other he knew. He was too hungry, and too joyous in the splattering blood, and bits of flesh to notice the strangeness of the thought.

The officer sagged, and Calian pressed him against the car twitching, and jerking like an insect to finish his meal. That's when he noticed the second officer, seated in the car, behind nothing but a blood-soaked sheet of glass. Their eyes locked, and Calian studied him in a moment of profound clarity. The dirty-blonde hair, the freckles sprinkled like nutmeg on his milky, ashy skin. Those young eyes – baby eyes, no more than eighteen – staring out at him in shock and horror and disbelief. There was no smugness in this one. Only terror.

For a long second there was an instant where they just stared, and then…

BOOM!

Calian felt the explosion in his shoulder, like a meteorite smashing upon an obsidian mound. Black shards mixed with flying glass erupted in a maelstrom, lacerating the arms, and hands of the first cop. Calian recoiled as a distant pain flooded his awareness, and he dropped the officer, who left a trail of viscera down the side of his car as he slid to the ground. The second cop raised the gun again, and terror filled the Ansect. With a roar that splattered them both with black gore and shards of bone, he bolted, and fled into the night. Sirens wailed as lights flashed behind him, and Calian found himself for the first time being hunted, rather than being the hunter. Still, he was more astounded than afraid, and already felt the mosaic flesh in his shoulder reknitting as he resumed his human shape. He still had sense enough to realize this would make him harder to find, so he sped up the process, though he knew the cost that would have.

It was not until he swept into his apartment complex, flew up the stairs, and burst into his room that he was able to feel his hunger again.

"Oh…." He moaned, as its terrible agony burned, and sizzled inside him. It was like a fire now, blackening his innards, and curling his intestines with heat. He clawed at his stomach with his puny human hands and twitched and writhed on the floor, shackled by pain that was almost beyond endurance.

I need to eat, he thought. *I need to feed. To feed. Meat, flesh, blood. Human bone snapped open, and sucked dry while I giggle and feed...*

In his hysteria, he realized his rage had left him, so that he felt sad, weak, and empty – yet, still blazing with hunger. He closed his eyes willing the pains to pass, fighting for control again over his urges, and his bloodlust. At last, his moans of pain faded into whimpers, and he was able to take his hands from his stomach and sit up.

I need to eat, he thought, and now that his rage had left him, he didn't care who or what his prey was; so long as it nourished him. He tried clambering to his feet and fell twice before succeeding. Then, as he stumbled to the kitchen to wash his face of blood, a great fear filled him.

I am weak, he thought. His human fingers trembled in the half-light, *I am weak. How can I hunt, when I am so weak?* Oh, the humiliation! How could he go back to the Hive and admit that these humans had stymied him, and weakened him to the point where he could no longer perform his task? *I will not do it,* he thought. *I will find someone to eat. I will keep looking, and looking, and when I find someone to eat I will gobble them down in an instant. Dear god, give me the strength to hunt,* he thought, and he was too crazed to remember that the Ansects had queens, not gods.

He made his way towards the door, feeling so dizzy he almost fell again. There was a whirling in the back of his mind like a swarm of bats. It was the knowledge that we would not be able to do it, he would have to admit he had failed, fighting against all those other fears to admit being heard. He closed his eyes to whimper and felt tears on his cheeks.

Then, he heard something that overcame all these other fears, and distractions. Three knocks, distinctly, on the other side of the door. There was a human being, outside, coming to see him; or, as he saw it, coming to their death.

"Hello, sir?" a voice queried. The voice was young. Feathery. Female. "Please, sir, if you're there, let me in."

Calian hesitated because that voice sounded familiar, and this made him suspicious. Still, his hunger won out over caution, and he opened the door. It was the female from the alleyway. The one Malcolm wanted to hunt. Even as he saw her, he felt a stirring of deep feelings inside his Husk that were alien to his Ansect self. It was akin to hunger, but it was nothing like Calian had ever experienced before. This furthered his sense of unease. What was she doing here? Why would she seek him out, after what she had seen? Was it possible that she *wished* to be consumed? There was strange prey like that, on the stranger planets of this galaxy, ones where he did not like hunting.

"What...do you want?" he asked. His voice was hoarse and guttural, presumably sore from all the heaving he had been doing.

"I wanted to thank you," she said.

Calian blinked. *Thank me?* he thought. What monstrous absurdity was this?

The girl heard his silence, took a deep breath, and repeated, "Please, can I come in?"

Calian wasn't sure. This was unlike any situation he had ever encountered. It occurred to him that this might be some sort of trap. His eyes scanned up and down the female's body, looking for secret weapons. That foreign hunger stirred in him again, and he stopped. Then again, even if she was armed, leaving her out there, with his door open to the world, seemed even more dangerous. His words danced on his lips where there used to be blood.

"You...truly want to enter?"

His stomach rumbled at the thought.

"Yes, please. Sir," she added at the end.

Calian bit his lips, urging his fangs to hide a moment longer, and stood aside from the doorway. She entered. Her movements were soft, and light- insectile, yes- of the beautiful insects. The winged kind, that rested upon flowers. The kind Calian would have to eat ten thousand of to feed him for a day.

Should I attack her now? He thought when the door had closed behind her. *No. I will wait to find out why she is here. Then, I shall consume her.*

"Thank me for what?" he croaked, his hands hidden in the folds of his coat. She smiled, and Calian marveled at the beautiful uselessness of the human's teeth.

"For saving me yesterday."

"Suh...saved?"

"From Malcolm, that terrible man," she said. "I think I must have fainted, because all I know is that Malcolm was there, trying...and then, I saw you attack. Did you wound him or something? I...don't remember much after I saw you pounce." Calian stared. Was it possible that she did not see him digest Malcolm's flesh? Could she really be that blind?

The human psyche must be beyond fragile, he thought, *to blot out something as normal as a hunt.*

"Malcolm will bother you no longer," he said, then thought, *in fact, very little will be bothering you soon.*

She took a step forward, and Calian couldn't help but recoil. All the thoughts of traps, and sabotage came flooding back to him. No prey stepped within arm's reach of an Ansect. Never. Still, she came closer.

"You see, my daughter, Lydia…she's a sweet sort, and naive. She became friends with one of the younger members of Malcolm's gang, and…"

Sweet. Naive. The words tickled his pallet as easily as *juicy* or *delicious* might have. This woman would be all of those things. Another step closer. Strange hunt, to have the prey stalking you. The woman trailed away, awkward and unsure.

"Well," she finished at last, "I just wanted to say thank you, for defending me. Most people wouldn't have done that."

This made Calian smile. She must have taken it as a smile of graciousness, for she mirrored the response. And then, she put her arms around him. Calian froze. Her arms were wrapped around his shoulders, and her neck was right next to his. A simple turn of his head would put him in touch with all those pulsing arteries. He began to shake with hunger, and she clung to him even tighter.

"It's okay," she murmured, and Calian could taste the moisture of her breath. "I don't even know your name." Calian grinned, and his teeth, like roots squirming to break through stone, at last burst free.

"I am Ansect!" He cried and buried his mouth in her throat.

****

That feeding was much cleaner than when he'd consumed Malcolm. Firstly, she died in almost an instant, disappointingly quick manner, for Calian's taste. That meant that she hadn't run and sprayed the city with her blood like Malcolm had. Calian did find out, as he sucked her dry, that her name was Teresa. Teresa and Lydia. Mother and daughter.

He did not stop to ponder long how he came about this knowledge. Gnawing at her body for nutrients was rather like sifting through mud for crustaceans. Who cared what interesting artifacts were unearthed? So long as little creatures continued to fill his belly. The major difference between consuming Teresa and Malcolm was that he fed on Teresa in his apartment, which meant that when the exhaustion hit him, he was already safe and sound. He fed so thoroughly that there was little evidence of her death by the time he was finished- except for the blood under his nails- chomping at the crispness of a final finger-bone, he promptly fell to sleep.

While Malcolm's mind had haunted him, he found Teresa's soothing. There was pain, sure – the loss of her mother, a painful farewell between friends – but most of it was as comforting as the ceaseless hum of the hive. Most of the dreams that greeted him were filled with images of Lydia – a young human of approximately eight years – though her age varied based on the dream. In many, she was nothing more than a baby, and if Calian had thought he was amazed at the fragility of the adult human, the infant child astounded him.

What a piddling lump of flesh! He thought. *To be swallowed in a single gulp!*

This reflection made his stomach twinge with an agreeable sort of contentment, as he continued to sleep through the pleasant comfort of Teresa's dreams. When he awoke, he felt well rested – that is, until the screaming started.

"Mamaaaa! Mamaaa!" he heard in his conscious brain over, and over again.It was a plaintive, and pathetic sound; yet sharp as shattered glass that filled the air with shards of pain, until there was no choice but to breathe it into his lungs. Calian's eyed darted like startled insects around his apartment. He was alone.

"Mamaaaa! Mamaaa!" Where was it coming from? He closed his eyes trying to focus, and clear as day he saw- as if it were in the apartment with him- the phantom form of a little girl. It was Lydia, and she was crying.

"Where are you, Mama?" The phantasm keened, holding her arms up in supplication. Calian knew the look. It was one his prey often offered him before they were consumed. But he had never seen it done while pleading for the life of another. It was alien to him, and he recoiled from it. He knew enough to sense he was no longer dreaming, and he ruled out the possibility that he was hallucinating. While he recognized that the image was not really there, every time he closed his eyes it erupted into his mind like flames; even after he opened to look, it stayed there, as if its bright light had burned his retinas.

"Please, Mama, help me," she pleaded. "I'm scared."

Then, the strangest, most disturbing thing happened. Calian felt a yearning in his gut; one unlike the feeling of hunger, or the rage he'd felt through Malcolm. It was as if something with blunt claws was trying to fight its way out of his stomach, and towards the crying child. For a second, Calian merely assumed that a twitching of life remained from the human he'd ingested and swallowed hard. However, the pulling, yanking, and scrambling feeling remained. This made him ill. Not like the shrieking agony he had endured through Malcolm, but a different, deeper nausea. He gnawed on his lips and dug his fingers into his stomach. Desperately fighting it back, striving to bury it beneath the satisfaction of the heavy meal he'd just had.

Images of his last meal, Teresa, conjured in his mind. Her flesh peeling away from blood- slick bones, the wet slopping of organs tumbling down his gullet, and the hearty snapping followed by the rushing of marrow as he cracked open a big bone; these thoughts were used as a shield of pleasure against the hateful nausea.

"Mammaaa? Maammaaa, where are you?" The voice restrained Calian's thoughts once again, and he turned, and vomited all over the floor.

****

Calian was frantic. Every meal he ate he could not seem to keep down. The strain of his own needs, as well as that of his Husk, were tearing at him. Hunger seethed, and when he was not hungry, nausea crippled him.

"I must find something I can eat!" he raged. "I must, I must, I must!" But what could he find? Malcolm had made him sick with anger. While Teresa crippled him by…something else; a longing, moaning emptiness, constantly howling to be filled. He could not find a name for it, but it reverberated through the ghastly shrieks of the no-child, the phantom haunting his mind.

That's it! He thought. *The child!*

How much simpler, how much less confusing must the flesh of an unformed human be? None of this sickness, this human nausea would follow if he consumed prey such as that! But where to find one? What little insight he had into the humans convoluted society told him that elder humans guarded their young ones well. It would be much harder than tracking a wanderer in a moonless alleyway, or eating the food that knocked at his door.

But, he realized suddenly, *what if one were alone? Unwatched? Uncared for?* He knew such a being existed, for he could feel it calling for help in his mind. Lydia. At the thought, a wave of nausea bowled him over, but he fought it.

I will consume her flesh, he told himself, *and then I will be sick no longer. She will be easy to find; because it's all here in my Husk, in my head.* Just as Malcolm's ghost was able to lead him to the cops, so too would Teresa's lead her to her child's. He waited until dusk, and then set off into the city. It wasn't far. Even as he slunk through the shadows, he saw a number of other human prey that he could have stopped and ate: gangsters, desperate woman, and smug men in uniforms; but he resisted. He knew that any of them, or all of them could make him sick. It was the child he needed, and it was the child he would get.

Teresa had lived in an apartment unlike his. Rather than row after row, and column after column of regular cubs, and white washed cement; this place was squatter, and made of brick. The squalid erosion of the brick, and the crookedness of the doorways showed that it was poor. However, those same aspects gave it character. For example, clumsy chalk wildflowers drawn and left by children filled the wall space; and the wilting herb gardens dangled from dented window sills. Calian glared at it all in disgust as he approached a doorway.

There was a small lockbox near the doorknob with his passage hidden inside. A strange Ansect or a human would not have known the code, but all Calian had to do was allow that strange longing to well up, that desire to be safe and sound inside. The knowledge then came upon him naturally. His fingers twitched over it like the legs of a spider, it clicked open, and revealed the key. A moment later, the door was unlatched, and swung aside. The apartment seemed empty. Orange light drifted through a lace-covered window from a nearby street lamp, lighting the small kitchen that was decorated in pastels. The few additions to the room included: fruit in a bowl on the counter, a sink inlaid with floral tile, and a single plate that rested in it. Calian saw crumbs on the plate, and smelt the toasted bread, causing his hunger to swell. Of course, this was not because he found it appetizing, but because it meant that there was someone recently in the house.

The longing filled his ears- less like a vibration, and more like a muffled hum- as if he had plunged his head underwater and listened. His whole body resonated with it, and he felt a throbbing in his gut.

Onward. Onward. He stole silently further into the apartment; he did not need to turn the lights on. His gut knew the place intimately. Through the living room, past the silent television that stood like a glass eye watching him, there was a worn but comfortable couch, and an image flickered through his mind. A woman with a child on the couch were laughing and braiding each other's hair. This made the throbbing in his stomach louder, and he quickened his pace. Down the hall, the bathroom had a tub with lining of rubber duck sticker, toting rain boots, and opening umbrellas. A family portrait- mother and grandmother- No man, but their smiles filled the vacancy. Then, Calian saw it, the child nestled in the mother's arms. His hunger growled at the sight of rich flesh.

Up the stairs, Calian was silent on carpeted steps, and continued past the master bedroom that still smelled like the woman that would never sleep in it again. Finally, he found himself at the girl's room. A wooden sign, done up in rainbows, read Lydia." There were some more stickers on the door that scrubbing with bleach had failed to remove. Calian leaned closer, and the smell of crayon was evident. He pressed his ear against the door, and what he heard thrilled him.

"Mama, Mama, where are you?" Cried a muffled voice that had the sound of breathing, and wet cheeks wiped on a pillowcase. "Mama, I called grandma. She says she's on her way." Calian hesitated, and then inhaled deeply. As he did so, his nostrils enlarged taking on an insectile aspect, and though he smelled a thousand thrumming human bodies close, he sensed that none drew closer. They were alone. He reached a bristling hand outward and opened the door.

"Lydia…" The word escaped him, like air from a cave- dank, moist, and terrible- seeking its fresh breeze. The girl gasped as she sat up on her little bed. Surrounded by green sheets, she looked like a flower-pale, and delicate- offering itself up from a blanket of leaves. She had always reminded Calian of a woodland creature, a fairy perhaps, with her little brown toes curled under her lap as she nestled that stuffed unicorn he had bought her at the fair.

What? Calian's mind shuddered. Where were these thoughts coming from? He wrestled them aside, and thought only of his stomach, and how even though she was so little, she would fill it. He stepped forward, and she cowered back in fear. "What are you doing here?" She mumbled, clutching the toy to her breast. "Do you know where Mama is? What are you doing?"

At the word, "Mama," Calian's stomach flipped. He took it to be hunger, and crept closer still. His teeth elongated forcing them to sprout out over his lips, and the claws of his fingers became blades that were as long as the child's forearms. She saw the bristled, barbed, spider-like weapons, and screamed. Calian pounced. It would not do to have her waking up the whole place. His neck shot out. His jaw unhinged, flapping like a terrible net to sweep her up and catch her. Lydia shrieked, and threw herself away from him. The unicorn slipped out of her hand, causing it to go flying through the air. Calian caught it on his teeth, and it split; thus, leaving tasteless, cloudy innards everywhere. Calian shook to free himself from the useless substance. The feel of fibers on his lips intensified his hunger, flooding his mouth with saliva until it dribbled down his chin to the floor. As if on continuous repeat, Lydia screamed, and screamed; and Calian's desire grew, and grew. It swelled up inside him like a fever, making his head swim with greed, and he lunged again, this time for the kill.

"Mama! Help!" The girl cried. Calian instantaneously froze. The last of the unicorn dust drifted to the floor. Something was happening to his stomach, and he could not move.

"No…" He moaned aloud, barely recognizable past the crowd of teeth. *No, no, no, no! Not again!* Sickness took him. He felt it rising from his stomach like a gorge, burning at his gullet, and souring the back of his throat.

"Mama help! Mama, help me!" The girl cried as she threw the blankets over herself; as if that would protect her. Calian saw the useless gesture and tried to laugh. However, all that came out was wheezing, and spittle.

"I must eat," he moaned, clawing outward. Lydia shrank, and the very tip of his claw alighted on her cheek through the blanket, thus drawing a single bloody tear. At the sight of it, his hunger bellowed, rising like a serpent from the darkness of the sea. For a moment, he thought it would win out, that this terrible affliction crippling him would quail beneath its awesome fury. But if his hunger was a sea serpent, then his sickness was the sea, for it swelled up higher, and dashed the both of them to the floor. Calian hit the carpet. His whole body shook, convulsing, oozing and twitching like a worm with a nail through its core. Terrible pain, unlike anything he had ever known held him in its grip. Hunger pains…he had dealt with those. They were terrible, too, but they had an easy cure. This pain…this sickness…this was an affliction of the species. His Husk, his prey – everything, he realized, was sick.

"Cursed species!" He moaned, and gorge flew from his flapping lips. "Cursed, weak, backward, twisted, broken species! What is this illness that consuming me – consuming all of you?" As he groaned, he took his own clawed, daggered hands and pressed them against the flesh of his stomach. Lydia, still terrified but silent now, peeped her head over the edge of her bed to peer at him, writhing on the floor. The sight of her eyes, wide and white as moons with terror, struck him like a spear in the gut, and he rolled away from her, clutching at himself.

"Someone help, please!" she cried. "Help us! Help us! Mama, what's going on?"

"Stop!" Calian bellowed. That word, *Mama, Mama, Mama,* wrenched and tore at him in a thousand deadly cuts. He actually felt as if something was *inside* him, clawing to get out, and he thought again of the *Cordyceps,* except that this time his terrible affliction was the parasite, and *he himself* was the husk, being consumed from the inside by the most terrible evil he had ever known.

"Mama! Mama! Mama!"

"Stop! Stop! Stop!" And then he screamed, "Enough!"

He erupted from the floor, gave the child a final look of abject horror, and fled the apartment, clawing at his innards the whole way. Mimicking overripe fruit, globs of blood, and organs fell from the hole he had torn in his stomach. Calian didn't even care that he was leaving a red trail of ooze with every frenzied step he took. He tore at himself, and tore at himself, wishing to get all the poisoned blood of humanity out of his veins.

Close by, sirens wailed. He did not hear them, nor the glopping sound of his insides splattering upon pavement. He was weakening by hunger, and pain, but the thought of what he had found in that house- the terrible feeling of nausea as he looked upon the child- drove him onward.

Out of this! Out! Out! Out! he thought, while thinking of his wretched human body, and his sickened, tattered Husk. He didn't care who was following, or about the screams that flew like carrion birds in circles above his path. His black claws dug inwards, striving to find the source of his sickness, and tear it out.

His apartment loomed before him, comforting in its symmetry, and in its ugliness. He flung himself inside, toppled up the stairs, where he found himself slipping on the stream of gore, and sinew that was trailing down into his wake. His door appeared before him. Bursting in, he was met with the impression of emptiness, and old sickness splattered all over the walls.

Out, out! he thought. *Out, out!* He strove to connect with the Hive, for them to rescue him from his body, and from this terrible place they called Earth.

Unexpectedly, he heard the soft *click* of the safety being drawn on a gun, and he promptly turned around. A man stood there, an officer, based on the coloring of his uniform. Calian's eyes widened as he laughed when he recognized the cop from before, the one with milky skin, nutmeg freckles, and terror in his gaze. The gun was pointed at Calian's forehead, and it was this that made him chuckle once more.

"No, no. No, no, no," he crooned, feeling the path of the bullet on his skull. "That's not the problem here, I don't think. It's this."

Calian reached upward. His stomach was an empty cavity, a hallowed place, like a crab stripped of its meat to be sucked with salt, and butter. He had already torn everything there out. Instead, he reached his taloned fingers further upward, beneath his shining ribs. There, his claw-filled grip found his heart, the shape and size of tender fruit, and he plucked. The gun went off. Whether it was his questing hand, or the bullet that killed him, his death sent him speeding back towards his Hive, and Calian would never know.

****

When Ian the Ansect finished downloading into his new Husk, his first feeling was of anticlimax, and then of excitement. *This? This is the terrible species that so many Ansect warned me about?* He eyed the weak, fleshy digits of its hands, the pallid, pink hue of its flesh, and laughed. *Some monstrous place,* he mused, still chuckling.

He ignored the stains of blood around the room and approached a pane of glass which offered him a view of the outside world. Below, he saw a multitude of meat-filled prey, just waiting for the hunt.

Humans, he thought in smug satisfaction. *Feeding here will be plentiful.*

PetER's Project

"What the hell, Peter? You think the Civs aren't looking? If they catch me near the badlands I'm fucked." Kora tossed her long, black hair as she flung off her helmet; her eyes burning a fire through Peter's face.

"You think I'd pull that stunt if I didn't know the location of every single Civ in a one-kilometer radius?" He asked, studying their surroundings with a sharp eye.

"It's not the eyes in the sky I'm worried about. It's your friend over there, Jim, who can't keep from drooling over my leather boots," she grunted in annoyance.

"Maybe you should change your outfit," he suggested with a wink.

"Maybe you should eat a big can of shut the fuck up."

"Come on. Jim's an ass, but he's one of us."

"No, Sim shop owner is one of us."

"I'm a Sim shop owner, in case you forgot," he reminded her hotly.

"You don't count," she snapped.

"And why is that?"

She shrugged. "You took this job because you had no other choice."

"I did have a choice."

"You made the only choice you could to save us, and I love you for that. What else were you going do to save your family?"

Peter inhaled, his eyes traveling back through time. "Max was a decent man, the best brother I could ever ask for. He told me not to take the job. I should have listened."

"There's no way you could've known what the Civs do."

Peter paused, clearing his throat. "Max knew, and in the back of my mind, I knew." He swallowed, forcing the sandpaper skin around his eyes to vaporize the tears before they left his tear ducts. Kora pushed Peter behind the Sim shop entrance curtain, which was decorated in Japanese, Chinese, and English characters. Korea would've emblazoned the curtain too if the country hadn't been annihilated in 2035 at the beginning of World War Three.

"You did the best you could, now suck it up before you draw even more attention than you already have."

"I told you, Jim doesn't care," he muttered, annoyed at her paranoia.

"He's on the take, just like the rest of them. Greed and hunger will make you do a lot of things to a man, especially slimy ones. Just look at his face. If a snake had a human body, that's what it would look like."

Peter rolled his eyes. "I've been watching Jim for years, ever since you were nine. He's never ratted out one of his customers, or mine. What makes you think he's going to start now?"

She pursed her lips as her eyes narrowed. "I don't trust him. I never did. No one important ever comes here. He never had a reason to rat out anyone. This time it's different, and you know it."

Kora pushed Peter behind the back room, he called it low-tech heaven. It contained every barely legal device to jack in. That's *all* the room had ever been, until Kora brought back the box a few days ago.

The shop's service bot rolled to cover the entrance for any incoming patrons. Kora unzipped her leather heels and replaced them with pink wheelies. She looped her long hair into two tight buns on both sides of her head and fastened them with hair ties. Then, she dropped down and retrieved the box; lifting the insignificant, shammy looking covering to reveal its contents.

"What are you going to do with that?"

"What do you think?"

It took a few seconds to register with Peter.

"You've gotta be shittin me! You can't. You're going get yourself killed," he exclaimed, reaching to try and take it from her, but she kept it out of reach.

"You can't protect me anymore Peter! It's my turn to protect you."

"And how are you going to do that? By getting us both killed?"

"I've been making this route every day for months. They've never stopped me. Security is highest here, and just at the edge of the badlands. If you don't pull any more stunts like you did earlier, I should be fine here. It's the outskirts I'm worried about."

"So, what's your plan?" Peter asked.

"The last two visits, I found blind spots in Civ network. I'm going to meet one of the rebels there. There's only one laser left after the rebels shot the other one down. The UN peacekeepers can't cover everywhere. I'll be safe in the blind spots, even if they have eyes in the sky."

He tilted his head back and forth, considering her words. "Maybe, but what about when you come back. If they see you, you won't be able to return. It'll be a one-way trip."

"Then I'll just have to make sure they don't see me with the rebels. And even if they do, I'll get you your medicine. Just stay out of sight. I'll give the signal over the back com once I make the exchange. You'll get your meds, one way or another."

"I'm getting old, Kora. You should let me go. I did what I needed to do. I don't want you risking your life for me."

"Don't go soft on me now. I wouldn't be alive if it wasn't for you. You might not be my dad, but I still need you to stay strong, especially if shit goes sideways."

Peter hobbled forward. He usually hid pain, but the injury festered. The last of his meds ran their course. He bandaged the wound well, but seepage leaked through the gauze and his trousers.

"You don't have the money to fix that," she said as she nodded at the spot.

"I can figure something out."

"Like what? Taking bribes from the Civs? Not sure you could even do it in your condition. I've made up my mind, so don't try to stop me," Kora said.

"When have I ever been able to stop you?"

"Glad that's settled. Stay out of sight. If the Civs see that wound, we'll both be a target."

Kora strapped on her quilted, patchwork backpack and enhanced rubber goggles. She stood out so much, that she blended in. She contorted the box into the backpack, then rolled towards the entrance. The service bot rolled out of the way. A few distant eyes peered in the Sim shop.

"Take care of yourself, Uncle," Kora said before vanishing.

Peter pulled up the screen from the refurbished television he had snagged from a recent scavenge. The last few digs uncovered newer tech, stuff Peter hadn't seen since EMP wiped out all the good stuff. Through the screen, he could see the difference in the alleyways behind the sim shop; he chalked it up to the destruction of the laser. He knew it worried a lot of people, while it gave others hope, but most of those were the wrong kind of people.

****

A tornado of dust slammed the shanty structures that lined the wasteland just outside the city remnants. Each structure was no more than six feet square, just large enough for each person to shit, eat, and jack in. Even in the desert, well beyond the makeshift city walls, everyone jacked in. Everyone except the Sim shop owners, rebels, and few remaining free thinkers that existed. Over time, most of them took to jacking in eventually.

There wasn't much else to do in New Texas, or anywhere for that matter. The rest of the old country was destroyed in the war. The new UN headquarters was situated in the dome in former New York City, erected before the bombs fell. It's hold on New Texas was tenuous at best.

The rest of the world was worse. A few cities in Europe remained: London, Paris, and Frankfurt. They controlled the remaining cities in the third world from the new UN Alliance.

The Rockies protected Texas. It wasn't destroyed by the war. It was destroyed by something worse: lost hope.

Kora peered through her goggles sizing up the shacks as she rolled by. A few bots eyed back. Over the next half hour, the shacks gave way to towering metal workshops. The smell of dry oil and tumbleweeds gave way to aluminum and sulfur. Even through Kora's goggles, the metal spray from welding blinded her to the tall metallic structures lining the flatlands all the way to the Rio Grande. She reflected on the contents of the box, the pristine surface that covered each face of the device. Its lines were sexy. A clear lacquer polished each side. Its design was efficient, whatever it was. But that was unimportant.

Kora didn't have the tech to pull it apart, but the rebels might. If she could take it apart, she could easily get enough green to cover the cost of Peter's medicine for a lifetime, and then some. She would never have to work again. It was safe in her bag. She dared not open it until she reached the badlands, no matter how bad she wanted to.

It was a miracle she pulled the box from where she did. The spot she visited every night scavenging, and so did everyone else who scavenged, had never revealed anything so promising. The box was prime pickings. Something that obvious was almost always taken by Sim shop owners' personal bots, which watched the spots continuously. Scavenging was one of the only illegal professions remaining that could bring in cash. The UN Peacekeepers turned a blind eye because they knew it lubricated the wheels of commerce in what remained of New Texas. And New Texas powered the economy of the world, as sad as that was. The UN hired the Sim shop owners to pacify the people, and they couldn't do that without the illegal tech that gave the real experience people needed to escape life after the war.

Kora approached one of the structures and wheeled in unnoticed. The factory bots could care less. They had one job: to produce. They made all the stuff everyone consumed. They grew all the food, they made all the smaller bots, and they made the legal gear to jack in. Food, shelter, and clothing were free, courtesy of the machines.

The UN gave everyone else a "living" wage of fifty credits a month. Medicine and equipment to jack in was the only thing people could buy with the credits. At least in theory. The city was in tatters. The machine bots couldn't keep up with the repairs needed, so people resorted to makeshift repairs. The illegal gear was made by the scavengers and the Sim shop owners.

Wheeled transportation outside the city was banned. Kora's wheelies where technically illegal, but not enough of an infraction for the peacekeepers to care. What the UN cracked down on were repairs, and structures. That was work left strictly to the machines. If the people started trading in repair parts other than jack in devices, it would upend the power structure.

A mid-level bot crept towards Kora.

"Whatcha got there?"

"Food, water, nothing to get your panties in a wad about," Kora replied.

"You're not allowed here. Leave or I'll force you to leave." The bot lifted its arm, pointing its gun at Kora's temple. "I said leave."

"I'm going. No need to get all defensive. What've have you got to hide anyway?"

The sound of the gun charging echoed in the expansive room.

"I said I'm going. See?" Kora said as she spun horizontally away from the charged barrel.

She took one more glance, as she knew the state of most of the bots. Only one was fully functional. Two more were partially functional. They hadn't been repaired in ages. The mid-level bot was clearly the peacekeeper's band-aid solution, which didn't require any human intervention but would last very long. It wasn't enough. By the look of things, the factory would only last a few more months at best. After that, whatever semblance of order there was within the cities would break down as people started trading black-market repair goods. People already were, just not in great enough quantities to upend things.

Visibility dropped as the wind picked up. Kora wrapped her face and neck with her scarf then pulled out storm gear from her pack. She'd have to take shelter from the storm until it passed.

****

Back in the city, Jim greeted an unexpected guest; her slim legs rose above his waist. He could tell she was angry and quickly directed her behind the back-room curtain.

"Did you consider my proposal?"

"I did, Felicia," Jim replied.

"And?" She sneered.

"It's not enough."

She scoffed in aggravation. "What I gave you was a generous, and one time offer."

"With all due respect, Madam Peacekeeper, I see what's happening here," he said quietly and calmly. "Everyone sees what's happening here. If you want me to risk my neck for the likes of you, I'm going to need a bit more incentive."

She pulled out her pistol, casually letting it rest on her lap. "How's this for incentive?"

"Now, now," Jim said.

Bots rolled up from behind and moved to Jim's side. An autocannon attached to the roof moved into position and aimed squarely at the peacekeeper.

"You think you can get away with threatening me?" She snapped, her eyes darting nervously to the bots, despite the way she squared her shoulders as if she was still really in charge here.

"No one's threatening anyone. I merely said your offer isn't good enough. You can pay me what I'm worth, or you can leave."

"My offer isn't negotiable."

"Yet here we are. I'm the only one that can get the job done, so you'll pay me my price or you'll get the fuck out," he stated with a smile.

"You're not the only one."

"I'm the only one that can do it right in the time you need it done. You can go back and get guidance from your superiors, but by that time it'll be too late. So, we're back to what I said before." He clapped his hands together as he grinned. "Pay me my price or leave."

Felicia grunted. "I need it done by tomorrow," she said as she transferred the credits into Jim's account.

"Pleasure doing business with you ma'am."

"It better be done, or I'll dismember your body personally and feed you to Tango." She warned hotly.

"That mutt's still alive?"

"Takes a lot of greedy Sim shop owners to keep him well fed." She leered at him as she stood, tucked her pistol away, and left.

****

The dust storm's brown wall receded, and Kora wheeled ahead. She was still miles away from the badlands. A few specks of black appeared ahead in the distance, nothing that concerned her yet, and so she pressed on. The thick blanket of dust waned and gave way to rotting flesh and vultures overhead that picked the bones of the stragglers who were unfortunate enough to get that far.

In the distance, two megastructures on each side marked the official border of New Texas between Seminole Canyon, and the Rio Grande. The border was pushed several miles north of the water to prevent residents from crossing. Not that there was anything left in Mexico, but UN Peacekeepers justified it as a needed deterrent to keep residents in check.

Kora eyed the broken laser. She assumed it was taken out by the rebels, but after seeing the condition of the machine shop, she took a closer look. The base of the laser was frayed and freckled with rust. Metal sheathing was bent where the hollow cannon tubing aimed at the target. She was still too far to tell if was decay, but it was a definite possibility. She wheeled faster, infrequently stopping to refuel on her meager supply of water and rations. It wouldn't be enough to last in this heat. She hoped it wouldn't matter as she was only a few thousands of yards away from the badlands. If she could make it to the Rio Grande, she could get enough for the box to cover all the rations she ever needed in cash, credits, or both.

****

When she had gotten a hundred yards from the Rio Grande, the ground shook. An army of bots appeared behind Kora, gathering quickly like a swarm of ants. Up ahead on and beyond the river, rebels amassed in even greater numbers. Kora picked up speed. She wondered if the mid-level bot gave away her position and sent a peacekeeper army after her, but it didn't make sense. She wasn't enough of a threat. Or was she?

Kora wasn't completely convinced she could trust the rebels either, but at this point, she didn't have a choice. The device was the only way she could pay for Peter's medicine, even though now she wasn't sure if she could get it back to him safely. The Rebels had contacts inside the city, but if she paid for a contact, she expected it would take every remaining credit after she bought the medicine. That is, if they even had the medicine. She only had one rebel contact, Alfred, an old school friend from before schools were disbanded ten years ago.

The armies stirred clouds of dust overhead, obscuring their exact location. The peacekeepers fired first. She didn't know why they called themselves peacekeepers. They were the ones who always fired first.

All she knew, is that like everything after the UN took over, it was a PR game to control the minds of the citizens. They accelerated the indoctrination program in VR. It was the only place they could after schools proved ineffective. It wasn't that they couldn't brainwash the students, it's that the process resulted in too many deaths. VR was simpler. People wanted to be corrupted in VR. By that point, they had already given up hope.

More shots rang out. The one remaining working laser turned and fired in the direction of the rebel army. It was too late. Kora found herself in the middle of the fight. She thought there was no way she could get anything for the device now. The rebels would take it by force. They had to. Fire from a laser pistol grazed Kora's side and she fell to the ground. She put her goggles back on, which gave her partial vision in the cloud of dust and smoke that rose in all directions. The rebel army scattered out of range from the remaining laser, but the bot army was almost on them and would surround the rebels in minutes.

The ground disappeared from under her. An arm pulled her down and to the left.

"Get the fuck off me. I'm warning you." Kora charged her pistol and pointed it at the humanoid figure in front of her.

"It's me, Kora. Geesh. Don't shoot."

"What the hell are you doing?" She snapped, aiming her pistol away before she hurt him.

"What do you think I'm doing? I'm saving your ass," Alfred grunted obviously annoyed.

"Well, what took you so long?"

"In case you haven't noticed, we're in the middle of a war," he said sharply with an arched brow.

"I can see that, but you could have given me a little warning."

Alfred closed the overhead entrance. Lights illuminated the underground cavern that stretched for miles. Before the war, coyotes used it for human trafficking into the States, and later the Republic of Texas after the breakup. The rebels expanded it, and from the looks of it, there were more rebels underground than citizens within the city.

"You know how things go out here. I had little warning myself. Did you bring it?" Alfred asked.

"Let me worry about the device. Just take me to whoever I'm supposed to sell it to."

He winked, leaning in closer. "You're looking at him."

"You've got to be kidding me," Kora said as she tightened her grip on the straps of her backpack.

"No joke. We don't have that many men as it is, so what you see is what you get. I can give you a fair price for it if it's as good as you say."

"It's better," she assured him. "I'm going to need enough to cover my trip back."

"You'll have to show it to me first."

"You don't trust me anymore?" Kora asked.

"I don't trust anyone, especially in the badlands."

She bobbed her head. "Can't blame you. But I'm surprised to see you go all badass on me. I thought I was the cynical one."

"War will do that to you I guess. Now quit stalling and show me what you've got."

Alfred led her to a large underground structure within the underground rebel city. They just made it there when another figure-head covered in a hood, face obscured by rags- stepped out from the wall, getting in between them. Kora froze, wondering what this was, but Alfred looked as confused as she was.

"Don't do it, Kora. If you do, you're not getting out of here alive," the hooded figure said.

Her gaze flickered from the figure to Alfred who shrugged at a loss. "And who are you? Why are you covering your face, and why should I care what you say?"

"You ask too many questions. You're just going to have to trust me. Don't give him the box."

The hair on the back of Kora's neck stood on end. She didn't tell anyone except for Peter the device was in a box.

"Don't listen to him," Alfred argued, trying to shove the man aside, but he didn't move far. "We need the device. You see how bad it is out here. We're making progress, but without those alloys, we don't stand a chance against the Peacekeepers."

The man barked a laugh. "You're a liar. You are the Peacekeepers. You're one, and the same."

Kora flinched at his words. "What the fuck are you talking about old man?"

The figure stepped forward. "I should know. I used to work with you," he added, turning to face Alfred. "That is until I figured out your game. You're two sides of the same coin, and you have the same leader."

"You're not making any sense."

"He's right," Kora replied. "You're not making any sense. The rebels have been fighting against the Peacekeepers as long as I've been alive."

"I know, Kora," the man said as he removed his head covering. "I should know because I'm your father."

Kora grimaced, taking a step back from this strange man. "I don't know who the hell you think you are, but you're not my father. I watched with my own eyes as the Peacekeepers killed you right in front of me when I was eight years old. My uncle Peter raised me ever since."

"That's only what we wanted everyone to believe. Not that I really wanted you to believe it, but because it was the only way to save your mother."

Kora hated games and she was in no mood to deal with some crazy person, not when she needed to get this sale over with and get out of there. "I'm done with this sick game you're playing, whatever it is."

"It's not a game," he insisted. "I'm alive and your mother's alive, too. It was the only way we could save you. We had to fake our deaths."

She shook her head fiercely. "That makes no sense. There's nothing special about me. But that's beside the point. I saw you with my own eyes."

He sighed, but it wasn't an impatient sound. "What you saw was a hologram. Admittedly, the best damn hologram that's ever existed, but a hologram nonetheless."

"How can I believe you?"

"Who do you think left you the box?" He asked quietly.

"No one left me the box. I found it. I scavenged it, like I do everything else since my dad died."

"I'm sorry Kora. I didn't want it to be this way, but—"

Shells rang overhead. Dust rattled in through the cracks from above.

"Follow me, Kora. I have something to show you," he said.

****

"I need that device, Kora," Alfred said.

"Whatever he's offering, I'll double it."

"And why would you do that?" Kora asked.

"I've had enough of this shit. I've tried to help you out because you're an old friend, but give me the fucking device. Now," Alfred said, pointing the gun at Kora's head.

"Sorry, Alfred," Max said as he struck Alfred's temple with the butt of his gun he pulled out from beneath his jacket. Alfred grunted in pain and fell to the ground, unconscious. Kora stared in shock as the man- who if he was her father was named Max- peeled the remaining rags from his face, and another figure stepped out from another room. She hadn't even noticed, too busy staring at the man that was clearly her father.

"Mom?"

Kora ran to her mother. It had been so long since she'd seen her dad, she'd almost forgotten how he looked. But Kora couldn't forget her mom's face. Lila spent every moment with Kora until she was eight.

"I don't understand. What's happening? What is all this?" She asked, pulling back from Lila.

"It's a long story, too long to talk about right now," she said with a soft smile. "But whatever you do, don't give the box to the rebels. It's more than just new tech or alloys for repairs."

"What is it?"

"Everything." She squeezed Kora's shoulders as she stared intently into her eyes. "It's why we faked our deaths, and it's what's going to stop the Peacekeepers."

"So, you're a rebel too?"

"Listen to your father. There's no difference between the rebels and the Peacekeepers. They're one and the same. It's a fake war manufactured by the UN to give the residents false hope. I'm not a rebel. We're on our own. We've had a little help here and there, but we owe allegiance to no one."

"Are you saying there's no hope?"

"There is, just not where you think," Lila replied.

****

Back in the Sim shop, Peter cleaned out his wound and reset the wrapping with his last piece of gauze. It would have to last him until Kora returned. If she returned. Chatter grew in the halls. Peter signaled the bot to put up the closed sign and watch the front room. Peter jacked in. It was his special sauce, a network reboot with an illegal tech and the only working five-dimensional simulator that existed in the city.

Everything in the outside world faded away. Peter never jacked it, but it was the only way to communicate with Max. The old system had background controls that kept people in check, but the new systems scrubbed the mind control and left the endorphin rush. Warm tingles spread over Peter's body. The pain from the wound transformed into the perfect heaven. Jacking in was stronger than heroin, at least from what Peter heard from the last of the junkies before the war. He would have scrubbed the endorphin rush too, but there was no time, and he didn't have the tech. It was a one-shot deal.

"You there, Peter?" Max asked through his headset gear.

"Smooth sailing. Smooth sailing," Peter replied.

The door shook.

"I think your friend's awake," Lila said looking over at Kora.

"What's happening? Why are you talking to Peter, and what are we doing here?" She asked.

Lila lifted her gun, and aimed it at the door. "Back the fuck up, Alfred," she warned with a frown. "What kind of a name is Alfred anyway?"

"Better than Lila. Now put the gun down and had over the box, or my friends over here will kill all of you."

Kora couldn't believe what she was seeing, but there was Alfred with several bots behind him, ready to attack. "What the hell? I've known you all this time and you're going to pull a stunt like this?"

"I wish things were different, but they're not. Now, hand over your bag," Alfred ordered.

One of the bots fired towards Max, the laser pistol grazed the headset, knocking it off.

"Max, you still there?" Peter said, calmly as his pulse slowed.

"Now you've gone and done it," Max said. "I was doing my best to play nice, seeing as how I knew your parents. Play time's over, motherfucker." In one smooth move he'd clearly done many times before, he detached the customized sawed-off shotguns strapped on his back, ducked down, aimed, and fired. Blasts hollowed out the bots, but Alfred was quick and slid out of the way, firing off a few shots of his own. Lila fired her pistols to cover Max as he reloaded, forcing Alfred to duck down, and she hit a bot behind him. He cursed and tried to move again, but she fired and grazed his shoulder as he yelped in pain.

"That's it, you little bitch," Alfred snarled as he fired back twice. Lila dropped, rolled, and tugged on Kora to head left with her father.

"I'm not going anywhere," Kora said. She unzipped her backpack, revealing a rotating quad laser, highly illegal and for good reason. Quad lasers were almost as deadly as the laser cannons.

It was Kora's pet project. She worked making the quad laser for the last year and a half, trading in whatever leftover scraps she could after covering the Sim shop bills and helping out Peter. The rest she improvised from old tech. She'd been missing just one piece, a small amount of platinum alloy that was non-existent in New Texas. Lucky for her, in addition to the device, the box also contained several alloy strips of copper, gold, nickel, and platinum. All of which could be used to power most pre-war devices or improvised new ones.

Kora aimed at the dozen bots that flooded in from the back, taking them out one by one.

"Kora, I need the device. Toss it over," Max said.

She kicked over the backpack to Lila and kept firing.

"I'm going to kill you, Kora," Alfred bellowed.

"Too late for that," she said.

Alfred charged the pistol, but Kora fired first, striking him in the chest. He died with a look of disbelief on his face, but there was no time to mourn a person she thought was her friend. As more bots flooded in, the three of them aimed at the door, using Alfred's body as a shield.

"I'm back Peter. Are you ready?" Max asked, having to yell to be heard over the noise.

Several dozen bots pushed forward. Fire raced towards the three of them as a blinding light filled the caverns of the underground city. Laser fire shot through the bots, but stopped short of the three of them. Kora dropped her weapons, watching confused.

"What the hell?"

The bots stopped firing, rotated their heads, and left the room. Just like that.

A second blinding light filled the room. A fraction of a second later, Kora and her parents were in a solid structure. Kora couldn't make out if she was underground, or some other building somewhere she'd never seen.

"What was that? I've never seen anything like that," she said, patting herself down as if to check all her limbs were still intact.

"That's what I was working on before the war," Max explained. "The company I worked for saw the war coming. All major governments were colluding together to force global control. I didn't know everything they planned, nobody did. All I knew, is it was no government I ever wanted us to be ruled under. I had a partial breakthrough just before the war, but I didn't tell anyone because I didn't trust what had just happened in my company."

"What breakthrough dad? What just happened?"

"I call it interphasic technology. It accesses the fifth and sixth dimensions of space."

Kora blinked trying to follow what he was telling her. "You mean like a parallel universe?"

"Not exactly. The device uses network technology to create holographic images, but those are real images projected through interphasic space."

"I'm not sure what that means," she said slowly.

"Quite simply, with this device, we can occupy the empty space of atoms. We can decide if people can see us or not. Either way, they can't interact with us physically unless they occupy that same phase state. And the only way they can do that is if they're in contact with the interphasic frequency."

"Holy shit," Kora whispered.

"Exactly."

"So, no one can touch us here." Kora paused. "Wait, who else is here with us, and why didn't you come sooner?"

"Glad you asked. To answer the first part of your question, more people than you think. We just couldn't transport anyone here until we were finished with the transporter technology. Peter's been working on that for a while. We had two missing pieces, and we couldn't reach each other across the border," Max said.

"So I'm assuming you're the one who destroyed the laser," Kora stated.

"I wish I could take credit for that, but it did play a critical part. As long as the laser was up, I couldn't get you the device. We've been waiting for Peter to finish the final piece of the upgraded network. That was what we needed more than anything else. With it, we could transport as many people as we could to interphase. That's what we call it."

Kora looked around. "Where are we exactly?"

"I told you we can access the fifth and sixth dimensions of space. The fifth dimension in holographic space, but the sixth dimension is very much like a parallel universe, one within our universe. Look out the window."

Kora lifted the curtain and saw what appeared to be the sun, but different. There were trees and rolling hills, a whole world that was similar, but different to our own.

"Welcome to your new home Kora," Lila said as she hugged her daughter. "Finally."

the Run

Traci perked up at the sound of her favorite show, she had just finished binge-watching the prior season, and this week was the final episode. She wore an obscenely tight, blue and red checkered button-down flannel, mostly to piss off her dad. After all, she was 18 now. So why couldn't she wear whatever the fuck she wanted?

"Dinner's ready darling," her mom, Samantha, yelled from the kitchen.

"You don't have to be so 1950's mom. Why can't dad cook for a change?" She complained as she stomped out of her bedroom to stand at the end of the hall.

"Don't talk to your mom like that, Traci. Be glad she cooks for you at all and that we have food to eat. When I was growing up—" Frank started to say- just home for work and still holding his briefcase- before he was cut off.

"I've heard this story too many times, dad," Traci muttered. "I know our grandparents were losers, and you were poor growing up. That doesn't mean you have to be a loser now."

Frank inhaled deeply, then held it a few extra seconds before exhaling. "I'm really sick of that attitude."

"I'm really sick of your attitude," she repeated in a mocking tone. "Why can't you just leave me alone for one freaking day and let me enjoy my show."

Frank shook his head and walked into the kitchen closing the door behind him. "I'm sorry, honey," he told his wife as he kissed her cheek. "I just don't know what to say to her. I don't know why she's acting this way."

Sam caressed his hand as he put his briefcase down on the table. "I think she broke up with her boyfriend. She stormed in here a while ago, and then she was on that phone of hers texting and snapping or whatever it is they do these days."

Frank peeked his head through the door.

Traci slouched into the sofa, tears streaming down her cheeks.

Frank turned back to Sam. "What happened?"

"I tried getting her to talk but didn't have any luck. Maybe we should use our secret weapon," she suggested.

"You mean Sean? I don't think she wants to talk with her brother right now."

"I don't think it could hurt, not with the shape she's in now," Sam replied.

"Alright then. You're the boss. I sure hope you're right because I'm not sure I can take another weekend with her all messed up again. Not after what happened last time."

****

Two hours later, Traci stood there soaked in the sweat from her skin; it completely drenched her clothes. She struggled to put one foot in front of the other. Her legs felt like she'd been working out at the gym all day and couldn't move another muscle; but she had too. It was the only way she could survive.

When she first arrived in the thick woods, she thought she was just being stupid and overreacting. She continued as she was intrigued by the smells of the sappy pine and decaying leaves. But then they followed, they were coming after her, and she couldn't hide from it. It was more than just her imagination; and they were really going to kill her. She was weak, slow, too much of a confused little girl who just broke up with her boyfriend to be able to run from, and fight whatever the fuck was after her.   It was impossible to keep up any sort of speed with tree stubs and fallen branches tripping her up every fifteen feet. She didn't understand how they could do it, how they could keep gaining on her. It's like they knew exactly where to place their feet before they looked.

They had done this before.

Traci tripped over the branch. Her legs collapsed, and her face planted squarely in a musty pile of mud and leaves. Her ears pulsated, almost drowning out the sound of what was coming after her. The speed of her breath was rapid, and the cool evening air burned her lungs the more she inhaled.

The rustling of the leaves and crunching of twigs grew louder. A few raindrops fell, turning into a trickle, and then a stream. The clouds blanketed the early night sky, covering up that last bit of light that illuminated the woods. With a gasp of despair, Traci clamored to her feet and ran. She forgot about how tired she was, the bad day she just had, and the good year she thought she had. All that mattered now was running as fast as she could, and getting as far away from those things who were after her. She tried her best not to look back. She didn't want to be one of those horror movie clichés who wasted the precious time they needed to escape by looking back, only to be captured in the act, and slaughtered to death. She wasn't a fast runner, but she had to get away.

A large branch snapped behind her. Goosebumps broke out on her skin. Her body trembled. She thought she felt something touch the back of her shoulder and felt a warm breath on the back of her neck. She ran faster, even though she knew it wasn't fast enough. She felt a cold hand clawing at her bare thigh, scratching her ivory skin.

Why was this happening? Two hours ago she was sitting quietly on the couch, warm and comfy on the couch....

****

The window shuttered. Traci shivered, opening the curtains to reveal the large black bird that just nosedived into the glass.

The television jingle momentarily arrested back her attention away from the dulling pain that came with losing her boyfriend. She sat there motionless for the next half-hour, enthralled by the twists and turns of the glossy, high-fashion drama.

"Good. Now that you're finished with that silly show, you can eat some dinner. It's already getting cold," Frank said.

Sam gave Frank a look that told him he had said something wrong.

"I'm not hungry," Traci mumbled.

"You need to eat something. You have a big day this weekend."

"No. I don't."

"You haven't forgotten, have you? You have the interview. I put my neck out for you, and I want you to do well," he reminded her.

She crossed her arms with a huff. "I've decided I'm not going to go."

"What do you mean you're not going to go? It took me two meetings to get that interview for you. I put my job on the line. You bet your ass you're going to show up," Frank said.

"Sorry, dad. I can't do it. I just can't."

"Listen, I don't know what's going on with you but—"

"That's right. You never know what's going on with me. Not that it matters. I don't care anyway. I'm not going, and I'm not changing my mind." Traci stormed off to her room and slammed the door.

Frank exhaled. "She's not coming out. Is she?"

"Afraid not. Just give her some time Frank."

"We don't have time. Her interview's on Sunday." He stared down at his plate for a full thirty seconds, and all he could think to do was shake his head. "You know, honey, I'm sorry. I just can't let her do this again. The last time she got in one of these moods she didn't come out of her room for two days, and I just can't have that. Not now. Not with things almost ready to go. She's on the rag, isn't she?"

"Frank! Be careful," Sam whispered. "I don't think most humans would say something like that. Not caring fathers anyway. Did you suddenly forget all your programming? Don't worry about your boss. He's plugged in. Things have been going well, and you don't want to screw up a good thing."

Frank was tired, tired of pretending to care. Tired of pretending to be a loving father when the truth was he hated that fucking bitch. He hated even more having to call her his daughter.

****

Blood dripped down Traci's thigh. If it had happened any other way, all she would have thought about was whether it would leave a scar. Her long legs were her best asset, and she liked showing them off.

She should be dead. She didn't know how she managed to keep going and run as fast as she did. She was already halfway through and if she could just keep going, if she should just make it to the other side, she might have a chance.

The air war was sharper now, cutting into her lungs each time she took a breath. She hated that feeling. That's why she never joined track, despite her dad's prodding.

The light was draining fast from the evening sky, making it harder for her to see in front of her. She moved forward desperately trying to avoid the obstacles that were waiting to trip her up and feed her to the beasts that were hot on her trail.

She still couldn't believe this was happening. She prayed it was a dream, but if by some slim chance it wasn't, she couldn't risk having those things overtake her. It just didn't make any sense. How come she couldn't see it before; couldn't see who they were?

Traci kept running, one tortured step at a time. But they were catching up to her. The sprint she made earlier was fading, and their steps were getting closer.

Her thigh exploded with the pain of a thousand needles along the line of the scratch where the beast's thick nails dug into her skin. She had never felt anything like this. The pain was seemed less real than the scales on the face of the horrible monsters who were after her. She couldn't let the pain stop her, she had to endure the unbearable pain. The kind of pain that would make her pass out on any normal day, would have to be overcome for today wasn't an ordinary day. This was life, or death. If she stopped, and she so badly wanted to stop, it would be over. She would be finished.

Their chase didn't stop. With every split-second thought, they grew closer, ready to pounce. What she did to them, how they turned, they would never forgive her. But that didn't matter. They weren't who she thought they were. All she wanted to do now was finish the job and bash their reptilian brains in until she was sure they were fucking dead.

****

Ninety minutes earlier, Traci was balling in her bed. She had wiped away the salty tears that dribbled down her plump red lips, so she could flip through her phone; devastatingly deleting images of her boyfriend who just broke her heart. She should have listened to the whispers about him, the rumors she refused to believe were true. But why did she have to be the one that he needed to figure out he wasn't completely straight? She didn't care that he liked boys. She just hated that he lied to her about it, that he used her that whole time just to prove to himself once and for all, that he was gay. It all made sense now, all the feelings and images in her mind from their past. She wanted to believe so badly he was straight. He was kind, gentle, loving, and did everything for her that she wished all the other asshole boys would do but never did.

But Mark was the worst of all. She gave him everything: her innocence, her virginity, and her soul. She told him things she didn't tell anyone. She told him about the time when she was five years old and didn't quite make it to the restroom because the front door was locked; she ended up emptying her colon on her front doorstep. That her dad was convinced she did it on purpose, and that the look in his eyes scared her to death. She thought he was going to kill her. But then her mother came out, picked her up, shit and all, and took her to the bathroom. Her mom washed her off until she was completely clean, then gently wiped away the mixture of tears and snot that covered her face from the most embarrassing moment of her young life.

Traci told him about the time she had her first period when she was eight. The doctor said it was normal, that girls were starting younger and younger, something about changing diets and milk protein. But all she remembered was being teased by the girls in the class. The bullying got so bad, the principal told her parents it would be better if they moved. So they did.

After that happened, she wanted to kill the principal and the girls that teased her. It just wasn't fucking fair. Life wasn't fair. She was the perfect little girl, and then some stupid shit happened, and it all changed.

Her dad never said it, but she was convinced that's when he started hating her. He hid it well, never hit her or anything, but she knew he hated her for making them have to move away from their perfect home. It was big, cheap, and the first real home her dad bought from the money he earned doing his important job he loved so much.

That's why it hurt as bad as it did, not that Mark liked shoving dick up his ass, but that he ripped out her soul and spat on it. She never told anyone any of those things. And there was more, so much more. She had even told him about the time her dad's boss came home for a work meeting; he was alone with her in the living room when everyone else was in the kitchen. There was something wrong about the way he looked at her. Maybe she felt it because she already started her puberty, but she knew it was wrong. He walked up to her like he was getting ready to grab her, even though her parents were just in the other room. He didn't even seem to care that her younger six-year-old brother was sitting on the couch. He was a fucking creep. He never touched her, but she was convinced he wanted to. She was so pissed that her dad was so stupid he couldn't see his own boss was a pedo. Now he wanted her to intern for him! She just couldn't believe it.

Her life was crashing down all at once. It made sense now, how her tortured friends at school could cut themselves to ease the pain. That's what she wanted to do now, just cut deeper down her wrists.

The pounding on the door interrupted her morbid thoughts.

"Get out here, now! I'm not going to tell you again. Get over yourself and eat your dinner. I just reheated it for you, and I don't want it to get cold again. Your mother cooked a great dinner, so don't disrespect her with that attitude."

"Leave me alone dad. You don't know anything. I hate you."

Outside in the hall, Sam tugged on Frank's arm. "Just let it go. She's not going to come out with you hounding her like this. She needs to come out on her own. I don't care about dinner. Just think about the first time you got your heart broken."

That *was* a long time ago, but it did the trick. Frank was twelve he when he broke up with his first girlfriend, much older than most boys; so, he let it go.

****

She was out of breath, and proud she made it as far as she did. She could see the lights of the house just outside the woods. It was a good thing. Moonlight wasn't enough to light the woods to keep her from impaling herself on one of the tree branches.

She didn't know how close behind they were. It took all the willpower she could muster, but she managed to forge ahead; and used all her strength to run faster without looking back. Even when the twigs and branches scratching up her smooth, milky skin, she kept going.

At this point, she didn't care if she was damaged goods. She didn't care that her boyfriend liked goddamn boys; and that she wasn't going to get another boy for a while in the condition she was in. All the boys she knew, except for Mark, were shallow pervs who cared only about one thing. She didn't want them, and she knew they weren't going to want her. She was the laughing stock of the school now.

It already started, the online posts with memes of her turning straight boys gay. One of the posts went viral and caught the eye of a classmate from her old neighborhood. They created their own post and tagged several of Traci's senior class. It was a post with an old photo of her and the words "Tampon Traci" underneath. Soon the secret was out; everyone in her senior class knew she started her period when she was eight. At least it didn't come from Mark. She would have had to kill herself then. At least it wasn't a meme of her shitting her pants when she was five.

But even the meme's didn't matter anymore, not with what was happening right now. She was almost killed by the creatures in the woods. She was convinced she was about to die and suddenly, suicide no longer sounded like a good plan. Only an hour and a half ago, Traci was seriously thinking about killing herself. All she could think about now was trying to survive.

Of course, there was the little issue of what happened after that. It just didn't make sense, but there was that knot in the pit of her stomach that told her something was wrong, really wrong. Traci had wanted to throw up the entire time she was running, but the adrenaline that kept her going prevented her from thinking about it. Now that she was almost to a house across the woods, the feeling of nausea surfaced with a vengeance.

Traci cleared the woods, taking expansive strides with her long legs. She was going to make it, she was going to survive. But she didn't want to leave anything to chance, so she kept going. Her feet hit sidewalk, and she turned the corner. She would be safest on the side of the house facing the street, where people could see her. The light was on, so there was hope. Traci pounded on the door, then finally allowed herself to glance towards the left side to see how close they were. It was a good thing she skipped dinner. Traci's mouth opened involuntarily, forcing out a yellow bile and half-a-glass of water from her stomach.

The creatures were nowhere in sight. Traci wiped her mouth with her arm as the door opened. "Please, I need your help! They're chasing me. They're trying to kill me. They'll be here any second. Please, just let me in." The boy stared at her perplexed. She recognized him from the neighborhood but didn't know him or his parents very well. They met a couple of times at a neighborhood BBQ when she and her parents had just moved in. His name was Jimmy. She wasn't sure if he recognized her.

"Please just let me in. Can I talk to your parents? They're going to kill me."

Jimmy stood on his tiptoes, cupped his hand over her ear, and whispered, "They aren't real."

A noise from the side of the house startled Traci. She pushed Jimmy forward, nearly knocking him over. She clamored to find the handle's lock, then slammed the door, turning the latch.

"What's going on? What happened to you?" Jimmy's parents asked worriedly as they came downstairs upon hearing the ruckus.

"Please, I need your help," she begged. "Call the police. Someone's after me."

"Who's after you dear?"

****

Traci's dad walked away from the door. Her stomach relaxed. She took a deep breath, crawled under the covers, and made the mistake of picking up her phone. It buzzed over, and over again. She ignored it for a while, not wanting to deal with the shit storm she knew was coming.

Notification after notification popped up on her screen. You have fifty messages. You have one-hundred messages. You have one-thousand three-hundred and fifty-six messages.

"What the fuck?"

Traci swiped the phone on and clicked the notorious app. Tag after tag, comment after comment, all saying the worst things they could possibly think of. She thought she acted slutty by comparison to some of the girls in her school, but she had a right to. It was her new persona after moving to her new neighborhood. It was her defense mechanism. She knew it, but she didn't care. It wasn't like she actually fucked all the boys in her school, but she had fun making some of the girls think she did. That was a mistake. She drew the ire from the most popular girl in school. Right now, at this very moment, it all blew up in her face.

"Bloody Traci." "Tampon Traci." Those were the main posts. Each had hundreds, some thousands of comments. Then, there were the snaps, and the tweets. Worst of all was the YouTube video that had over eighty-thousands views with a banner comment at the bottom giving a link to Traci's nemesis, Crystal's, online page. That's where she saw the post roasting her as "Tampon Traci."

This was a time for the special bottle of vodka she snuck out of her dad's liquor cabinet. She usually only had a little mixed with something super sweet, so she could drown out the taste of alcohol. Not tonight. Tonight, she chugged it. She needed something to make this go away. If she had a crack pipe, she would've smoked it. At least her asshole father went away. She wished she could go away. For the next half hour, she couldn't keep her mind from racing. Finally, the alcohol and mental fatigue wore her down. She passed out, letting the bottle roll from her bed, shattering on the floor.

Traci woke to the door pounding.

"Traci, what's going on in there?"

"I'm fine. Just leave me alone dad," she said, trying not to slur her words.

"You're not fine. I heard a bottle break and I noticed a bottle of my vodka is missing."

"Just leave me the fuck alone okay!" She yelled. "I don't care anymore. I hate you. I hate my life. I want to die right now. Just go away."

"Open this door now, or I'm going to knock it down," Frank said as he pounded again.

"Leave me alone," she replied.

With that, Frank let loose. It took a few tries, but he shouldered his way into the room, ripping the door halfway off the hinges in the process.

"What the hell are you doing drinking in our house?" He stormed.

Traci lost it. She charged Frank, pounding at his chest, crying all the while. "Let me go. Let me go," she shouted, continuing to pound on his chest.

Sam stepped towards Frank. "Let me talk to her Frank. She's just being a teenager."

"I don't care if she's being a teenager or not. She's drinking in our home and acting like a hooligan. I don't care if she just graduated or not. She still has to live by our rules."

That reminded her of the silver lining, the reason she didn't immediately kill herself. She did just graduate, which meant at the very least, she wouldn't have to face that bitch, Crystal Gatewood, the next day in school. But it was also the reason why Crystal could be so vicious. The school had a strict policy on cyberbullying, but there was nothing they could do now. They already graduated and had their diplomas. High school was over. But it still managed to come back and bite her in the ass.

"We're going to talk about this Traci, now. You're going to sit down, and you're going to tell me what the hell is going on."

****

It was a good thing she finished off the bottle of vodka. Otherwise, she wouldn't have had the stupidity to pick up the bat that her brother left leaning against her wall. She didn't mean to, but before she knew it, the bat was impacting her dad's head. What the hell had she just done? The bat had barely made impact with his skin before she already regretted what she did. If her life wasn't over yet, it surely was now. Any second, her father would have a huge bump on his head and be crashing to the floor. The police would come and take her away to jail.

The only thing was, that wasn't what happened. The bat struck her dad in the head, hard. Only, there was no blood. Instead, she saw a bit of green from the silicone skin she had damaged.

"What the hell?" She blinked, confused, and wondered if she had too much booze that was making her hallucinate.

Frank smiled, touching the green scales on his face that now peaked through fake human skin. "I wish you really hadn't done that Traci. I know things have been a little tough lately, but we could have fixed that."

"What are you going to do?" Sam asked as Traci stared from one to the other, horrified.

"It's too late now. We're going to have to start over again. Wipe her. Give her a clean slate."

"I wish you wouldn't do that. We still need breeders."

Traci's eyes widened. Her mouth gaped wider. She knew this thing wasn't her real mother. She didn't know who the fuck her real mother was, or what happened to her real parents if she even had any. Did it happen when she was eight? Was that real? What the hell happened, and what were these things in front of her? Traci picked up the bat again and struck Frank harder in the head. Strike after strike, she pounded at his head until most of the skin was off.

Frank laughed.

"We might as well show her who we are now. She won't remember any of this anyway," Sam said.

Traci didn't know if these green alien fucks had the same private parts as humans, but it was the only play she had. Moments later, she kneed Frank in the groin.

"I guess that answer was yes," she said aloud, feeling vindicated her plan worked as he doubled over in pain, spitting curses at her.

It didn't take long for her to make it to the back door and bolt outside towards the woods.

What the hell was going on? Traci wished she had drunk two bottles of vodka. She needed it.

The door slammed behind her. The back-porch lights came on. She stumbled, jumped back to her feet, and never looked back. She hated the woods, especially at night. She was eighteen years old, but still frightened of the dark. She knew she was too old to be afraid of silly little things like that, but she guessed now she was right to be frightened all along.

The woods were foreboding, but no less terrifying than discovering both her parents were actually green reptilian aliens who wanted to impregnate her with reptilian eggs.

****

Jimmy looked out the window.

"Do you see them?" Traci asked, terrified they were still out there.

"See who dear?" Jimmy's mom asked.

"Two people were chasing me. They're trying to kill me."

"Who's trying to kill you?" His mom asked calmly.

"I don't know exactly. All I know is that they're coming for me. Just close the curtains so they don't see me inside, and call the police," Traci begged. "Please!'

The house phone rang, and Jimmy's mom answered, nodding her head.

"I told you," Jimmy said with a sigh. "You should have listened."

Jimmy's mom looked down at him. "What have you been whispering in this little girl's ear? You know you can't be scaring away our breeders like that, don't you?"

Traci jumped back, fumbling again for the doorknob. From the corner of her eye, she saw through the curtain that the reptilians were approaching the door. Jimmy's parents stepped forward and grabbed her wrists just as the front door burst open. Frank and Sam forced her down onto the ground. "Grab the wiper. She's no use to us like this. We can breed her later," he said. Traci fought back the best she could, but slowly they pinned her to the ground further, limiting her movement.

"It would have been so much easier if you would have just listened to me and come out of your room. The internship would've been good for you."

"Fuck you, you alien motherfucker," she bellowed.

Sam put her hands over Traci's eyelids, forcing them down. She bent down and whispered in her ear, "It's going to be okay, sweetie. You won't remember a thing."

The light that bled through Traci's eyelids went black. Her head spun, and she passed out.

She wasn't sure how much longer it was, but she heard her favorite movie playing on her laptop. She opened her eyes, lying on the floor by the side of her bed, gripping the bat that was under there.

"You okay, Traci?" Frank asked, standing in front of her.

"Get fuck away from me," Traci shouted as she pulled the bat from under her bed and started swinging.

"What the hell are you doing? Have you been drinking? You're going to hurt someone with that, now put the bat away," Frank said as he maneuvered his way in to try and grab the bat.

But it was too late. Traci made contact and struck his head as hard as she could, then swung the bat towards Sam. She closed her eyes and kept hammering away at both of them until she heard the crack of both their skulls.

When she opened her eyes, all she could see was red everywhere. Blood and brains splattered against the wall, and then her brother walked in screaming.

Traci collapsed on the floor.

Twenty-minutes later, cops swarmed her house. Multiple squad cars lined outside her home. They hauled her away in cuffs. The last officer that left her room turned off her laptop just as the credits rolled up.

"One eight seven Roger. We have the girl in custody," the female officer said as they exited the home and entered the squad car.

the WRENCH & tHE BOLt

We were nearly past the barricade when the first bomb struck us. When you're on land, free in the air, or bound by an oppressive steel ceiling; explosives light you up with hot air and a swift percussion. It's terror for an instant, and then it's gone. Leaving nothing more than flickering flames and memory.

When you're underwater, as we were, it's something entirely different. The sound of it was strange. There was a delay, a deep, muffled, thump as it struck the outer hull. Then, a hesitation where the impact shuddered through the entire vessel. Finally, the explosion: less like a singular burst of energy, and more like the hand of God sweeping down and slapping us silly. The whole submarine rolled, bucked, and swayed with its force. Men tumbled, and bags of provisions slammed against metal walls causing tiny explosions with each hit. Hands, knees, and elbows were cut as my crew strived to catch themselves and restore balance. Still, the sub trembled.

After the final quake, I ordered all of us silent. We turned the engines off, no noise would help hide us deep in the silence of the water. It would seem strange to the outsider: calling everything to a halt and sitting like a wounded duck after a single hit. But the true strength of a submarine lies not in its weapons, or in its formidable hull, but in its ability to hide. To sink into the safety of the depths like a crocodile into the muck.

We could not survive an open encounter with the ships above. We must lurk below them and wait. It was a good plan. It had saved us many times before. At the Mediterranean, Svalbard; we hid and bit our fingers, sucked our flasks, and tried to quiet the thrilling, hopeless terror threatening to burst out of each of us. That's the worst of it, I think: being so consumed with fear with absolutely nothing you can do about it. I thought there could be no worse sensation.

That is, until the second bomb hit us, and our engines imploded. I felt the damage like an earthquake, and with the sudden heaviness in the back of the sub where the engine room resided, the whole craft tilted. I was thrown to my knees while the screams of horror from my men swarmed about my ears like bats. I reached out, clutching at pipes, and gazed in abject terror at the pressure gauge.

We were sinking. The engines were dead, and we were sinking. Perser, the medic and my close friend, burst into the control room. His face was pale and ashen, barely visible in the red emergency lights that illuminated our little steel world.

"Captain!" he exclaimed. "Harper and Jones are down, concussed during the impact. Mason and Gerard are trying to get into the engines, but the ways are sealed, and…"

He paused, noticing my silence, and how my eyes were not looking at him.

"We're sinking," I said.

He licked his lips. "Sinking, sir? I…I haven't heard the engines…"

"Look," I said.

His gaze found the pressure gauge.

Eighty meters…one hundred meters…one-hundred and twenty meters…

He watched the needle go downward, and a bead of sweat rolled from the corner of his eye to his jawline. Or maybe it was a tear?

I glanced behind him. My words had traveled through the sub like our torpedoes through the water, seeking out the peace of mind of every man on board. They crowded around the entrance to the control room, folding themselves into bunks, slipping behind boxes. Dozens of eyes gazed up at me, imploring and desperate as wet kittens.

"Captain Valence…what should we do?" Someone asked. It was Thomas, not three months past eighteen; most of it spent underwater. Being the youngest male aboard – I hesitate to use the word "man"– he was the only one known by his Christian name, rather than by his surname or role. He looked especially young right now, crouched among his bed in the corner of a bunk.

"We maintain silence," I said, "and if you wish to pray, pray."

I wouldn't be praying. This long war had exhausted whatever patience I'd had for it. But I would not stop the children. That's how I thought of them. Children.

The submarine descended. I heard her metal skeleton creaking and groaning like dead trees in the night. *One hundred eighty meters...two hundred meters...two hundred twenty meters...*

No banker or gold monger in all the world has ever watched their numbers rise with such intensity. The groaning grew louder. I heard my heart beating in my eyes, imagining the thunder of exploding metal and the rush of water that would kill us in an instant.

Perhaps it wouldn't be so bad, I thought, over the rumble of the sub. *A shock of noise, followed by death. Not such a bad way to go, really.*

However, as I gazed around at my fellow men, my soldiers, my Tommies, fighting in a war they did not want, I realized not one of them shared these comforting thoughts. They were terrified and were right to be. Down, down, down we descended. The water developed a pulse, and I imagined us alive and sealed inside a bean, in the belly of a giant beast that soon would devour us completely. I waited for it. That quick smack of pain, then oblivion. Waiting...waiting...

Baul-loooom.

The engine room filled with water as the heaviest side had struck something solid. Everyone screamed. Boxes jolted and burst open, and Thomas fell from his bunk. Perser was beside him in an instant, checking a small cut on his cheek. For my part, I checked the needle of the pressure gauge.

It had frozen.

For better or for worse, we had stopped.

"Thank God!" someone shouted.

"Praise Mary and all the saints," another cried and let out a loud whistle. Funny, how a group of men who drink, smoke, and consort with whores at every docking; suddenly turn religious when their fear pounds louder than their dicks.

"Thank the stone beneath us," Perser muttered, who stood immediately to check on Harper and Jones, injured earlier.

As for me? I thanked no one, for though we had stopped descending, our danger was just as great. Then, as if to prove it, the first bolt burst.

TWANK! Pssssssst!

An explosion of metal, a broken bolt rocketing through the air as fast and deadly as a bullet. Water hissed through its fractured place so quickly it was almost steam, and again my crew erupted in screams.

TWANK! Pssssssst!

TWANK! Pssssssst!

One connected, hitting Davis square in the throat leaving a hole so big I could have slipped a grape inside it. Blood gurgled out of his mouth, and then he, and the globules toppled to the ground.

"Perser!" I screeched. "Perser! Perser!"

But he was already at Maloney, bleeding from the shoulder.

It was time to take command.

But why? My mind interrupted suddenly, like the nagging for a drink. *Why bother? Who cares if Davis bleeds out? It's that or drowning anyway. Pick your poison.*

But it was not my job to think such thoughts. That was for the field marshals and the generals, choosing the method by which their men would die. I was a captain. When my men died, I died with them, and that makes it another matter entirely.

"First watch, port! Second watch, starboard!" I thundered over the hissing serpent tongues of water. "Third, engine room! Seal it closed, now!"

Like a flock of startled birds, my men leapt up and wove around each other to close the leaks. Wrenches, fresh bolts, bloodied palms, and shredded fingernails; all worked together to seal the bleeding, creaking, groaning, screaming carcass of a submarine.

Water started rising from the floor, black with grit where it wasn't red with blood. It covered my boots, and for the silliest of moments I childishly watched the stream of water I created; flowing around me so peacefully.

Then, I turned towards the engine room to help the third watch at their task. The engine room was finished, but under multiple feet of smoking water. Machinery, and hope; both swallowed by the sea. I had made the decision already. *Seal it closed. Don't fix it. Seal it closed. There's nothing we can do.*

That was precisely right. There was nothing we could do. Water rushed into it. It was already heavier than the rest of the craft, pinning us down in a slant. I and three other men managed to slam its door closed, and the rush of water broke against it, helping us be strong. We turned the bolt by hand, but it was not enough. Water leaked through; we weren't strong enough to manually seal it tight. Suddenly, Perser was beside me. He handed me a wrench, and I locked it into the curve of the bolting mechanism.

We strained. I strained. My men strained. Until, finally, the water stopped.

Behind me, only a trickle. A few swipes and minor swears were all we needed to stop the rest of the ruptured bolt holes from leaking. My men sagged in exhaustion- but not relief- onto their bunks.

Eerily, a ripe banana and a few stray cards from a deck of naked ladies floated by. A slight current brought them together until they touched. Perser, Thomas, and the others close enough saw this and began to giggle. Men raised their eyebrows and pointed, and the laughter spread like a disease across the whole of my boat until every crew member was rolling, shaking, and trembling with laughter.

Every last one, except me.

Ask any sailor. One man's sickness is always everyone's sickness; from the flu to little biting crabs. Except the captain. Every bitter seaman will say that, somehow, the captain always escapes.

I suppose it is true for merriment, too, for, as I watched my men, ankle deep in water, sweat pouring down their faces and their uniforms so stained they were the color of the sea, I saw nothing at which to laugh.

****

It got cold. Usually, on a submarine -even without any deliberate heating- it was hot and sticky as the Malaysia jungles in which our brothers fought. Upwards of thirty men crammed as sardines, working, sweating, and stinking in the confined space.

But now, everything was motionless. The engines dead, my men listless, waiting. The temperature continued to drop until we felt the cold creeping into our clothes, beds, and thoughts like some sickly, unwelcome lover. I thought and thought about how to get rid of it, but the pumps were broken, and there was no way of returning it to the outside. Finally, Perser had the idea of taking much of his emergency medical supplies – the bandages, in particular – to soak up some of the excess flood.

It helped. A little. He made sure to keep plenty for Davis and Maloney. If I had to bet, I would guess that Davis was not longing for this world. If I had caught any of my crew members taking bets, I would have bashed their heads against the interior hull, to hell with court marshalling. Maloney had a chance of making it; well, as much as a chance as any of us.

The longer we waited, and the colder it got, the more people realized that there was absolutely nothing we could do.

"Cheer up, chaps," Perser said, always ready to offer a smile to dying men. I didn't know how he did it, always grinning when blood, gore, bombs, and water flew. *Perhaps he is insane,* I thought. *Perhaps I am.*

"Don't worry," he continued. "That was a heated battle up above. Our boys in the destroyer were bound to have noticed. Soon, they'll be down here to rescue us, you'll see."

No one contradicted him. Why bother? If he was wrong, as I knew he was, it would prove itself in time. Either way, the men were desperate for comfort, and soon clustered around him the way I have seen small children do. I hung back, fading into the shadows, a forgotten reminder of our plight.

"Relax, everyone," Perser urged. "Captain Valence has gotten us out of far worse messes than this. Remember that time we came up in that fog and there was a destroyer right there?"

"A chicken to our egg, that was," somebody said with a chuckle, and then someone else said, "a *dragon* to our egg, more like."

Perser smiled. "How about when we all got the fever, and Valence guided us all home in time for the antibiotics?"

"Hear, hear!" someone called. "Hell, Harper was hallucinating a mile a minute that week. He kept calling me King George VI!"

People chuckled. The sound didn't travel far. The air was too thin and heavy. A strange mixture, half water, half suffocation.

"If anyone can get us out of this, Captain Valence can," Thomas declared, and each of his words were like ice in my heart. *They really think of me this way,* I thought. *They don't see that I'm scared as shitless as they are, and just as lost.*

I took a deep breath, then fought back panic when I realized I was just as breathless as before.

"He'll get us out, all right," Perser assured the men. "He promised my wife he'd get me back to her and my little girl."

"You sure that's the *only* promise he made to your wife?" Someone said, elbowing Perser, who ignored him.

"Yes," he went on fondly. "Little June will be going on two now. And she's getting so big! Look here."

He pulled a photograph from his pocket and showed it around. It was so tattered and worn that we may as well have been looking at a gray smudge on old metal, but of course no one said that. Instead, they oohed and ahhed and stared with glistening eyes at the image.

"She'll be a beauty one day, just like her mother," he said, and there was a collective mutter of agreement.

"I just got my brothers waiting for me back home," Thomas said, taking up the cue. "I'm the only one old enough to go off to war, and they'll want me to tell them all about it."

Though I knew that already, this reminder of it gave me a little shock. It was hard to imagine Thomas as older than anything. He seemed the youngest creature ever to exist. For some reason, this brought tears to my eyes, and anger to my heart. It could have been the air. It was smoky and biting, and everyone's eyes were red and swollen. It could have been that, but it wasn't.

I breathed again, and each time found it harder.

"Well, *I* ain't got anybody waitin' me," another man offered, "but a whole city of greater hookers a-looking to welcome a soldier home!"

A hearty laugh followed, rude gestures and shoved shoulders. I whirled away; for some reason their laughter disturbed me. Instead, I glared at the motionless depth gauge, struggling to control my anger- to keep it from quickening my breath – and slow my suffocation. Perser must have noticed, for a moment later he was up, and circling to the control room to speak to me. His movements were stiff and painful looking; I could tell that the cold, and lack of air was getting to him.

"Davis is dead," he whispered. It sounded like rubber slid across wet gravel. "He died about an hour ago. I didn't want to tell the men until you...well, until we figured out what to do."

I turned around and stared at him. He was a small man, and by glancing over his head I could see into the bunks where most of the men waited. There, on the far bunk, under a blood-covered sheet, lay the body of Randall Davis, unmoving. For a second, I was surprised that none of the other men had noticed. Then, I realized as the lack of air scraped at the raw flesh of my lungs, that no one was thinking about anyone's breath but their own. Each one of my men's ribcages barely fluttered. I was not worried about the smell, or the rot. We would all be log dead from lack of air or implosion before the body's putrescence could harm us. In a shuddering thought, I realized I was jealous of Davis.

"Dead, then?" I hissed. "Well, he's the lucky one. Going out with a quick and honorable wound to the neck, while the rest of suffocate and freeze to death!"

Perser's eyes widened. "Sir?"

"Don't you realize, Perser, that *there's nothing we can do?* The engines are dead. The pumps are dead. Davis is dead. Everyone is dead.

And we're just the ghosts, telling stories about old lays and sweethearts!"

As I spoke, my voice rose, loud enough to carry to the men. They glanced over, eagerly, as if waiting for me to bark out an order. Instead, I shouted, "He's the lucky one, you hear? The lucky one!"

Immediately, Perser grabbed me by the arm and led me deeper into the control room, shutting the door behind us so there was nothing left but him, me, red light, and the single, gleaming eye of the pressure gauge. When he spoke to me, it was gentle, as one would speak to a frightened animal, or a child.

"Are you okay, sir?" he asked. "Perhaps you would like some medication? We have plenty of morphine. Perhaps just a small dose or two, to calm you down…"

"Morphine," I echoed. The word hit me like a ray of light down in the dark, dark, depths. "Morphine…Morphine. Truly, we have plenty?"

"Our men have been lucky, sir," Perser said proudly. "Very few injuries until now. We have quite a stock."

"Good. Bring it to me."

Perser opened his mouth in protest, realizing that, if we were all aboard the boat, I was still captain, and then went to retrieve the drugs. He returned a moment later with a satchel, which he opened to reveal dozens and dozens of syringes; little syringes filled with a dying soldier's sweetest bliss.

"Is it normal, to carry around so many?" I asked.

"I trained in infantry, remember," Perser said. "Plus, on a submarine trip…who knew how long we'd be out? Or what sort of injuries our men would have to endure, or for how long? They made sure we were well supplied."

Who knew? Would have? We were? All these past tenses. Perser did not notice, but I did. That was the captain's job.

"How much for one?" I demanded.

Perser shrugged. "In the field, for the truly wounded, a single Syrette suffices. For you…just to calm down…an eighth of one? We want you lucid."

Lucid, yes. I was feeling more and more lucid every minute, in spite of the nagging exhaustion of the rotten air, and the cold slipping slimy fingers on my bones. I was more lucid than any of them.

Perser's eyes twitched from me to the case of syringes, feeling nervous. I knew this must be strange for him. He was not being disingenuous when reliving my heroic moments with my men. He truly believed them. And now, to see me so disturbed...

It was as if I could read his mind. *Things really are bad, for the captain to be so upset,* his nervous brow said. I took this as confirmation. Yes, things were bad. I knew it. Perser knew it. Hell, even Thomas the kid knew it.

"How much for a lethal dose?" I asked.

Perser started. "Oh, sir. I wouldn't worry about that."

"Still," I insisted. My voice was as deadly quiet as the engines.

"Well, in normal situations, a man can take several. But if you are wounded, or sick, or drunk—"

"Or suffocating."

"Then the patient would be unconscious with two. Possibly fatal."

I smiled. It was the first smile I'd offered my men since that first bombing. "Perfect," I said, and snatched the satchel from his hands. He stared at me in astonishment as I rose and strode directly to the hatch.

"Wait, sir! Sir! What are you doing?"

"Silence, Lieutenant Perser. That's an order."

He quailed, and I marched past him.

The men jumped at my entrance with their eyes. Their bodies were too tired to react. I saw one, Johnson, stuffing an unlit cigarette in his pocket in embarrassment. I went right up to him, took the fag from its hiding place, put it in his mouth, and lit it.

"Go ahead, Johnson. Enjoy."

The man smiled, and inhaled. A moment later, thick tobacco smoke unfurled from his lips and filled the air. In all my long life I had never smelt anything so delicious.

The men breathed it in too. To taste, smell, and breathe anything other than the dankness of the rotten air was beautiful.

"Anyone got booze?" I asked, and in answer I got a small cheer. Men ruffled through their sodden sheets and pulled out flasks, bottles, and pouches. I ordered the cook to break out all our stores; whatever wine, vodka, and whiskey we had.

Soon, every man had a drink in his hand. All except for Perser, who hovered behind me like a worried shadow, and just as helpless as one.

I raised my own wine, red. "To the Moorhen!" I said, naming our epithet for the sub. Everyone followed suit; smiles and laughter trickled from their mouths like smoke under a door. Then, I reached into the satchel slung over my shoulder, grabbed a pair of syrettes, and tossed them to the nearest man. He caught it instinctively; it was tossed to the next man, and another, and another. It didn't take long- like handing out candy at Christmas- they held them up to their eyes, some in confusion, and many in dawning understanding.

"We are trapped down here," I said. "Our engines our dead, and even if they weren't, our pumps are dead. There is no way to remove the water from this craft. We will never see the surface again, nor breathe its sweet air."

I paused, letting my declaration sink in. A few – Thomas among them – stared at me in horror and disbelief. But the older men – the ones who had seen many battles, and many deaths – showed gratitude in their eyes. There was a rustling as they began opening their syringes.

I continued, "without help, there are two ways we could die. The hull could finally fracture, and the water would rush in, killing us instantly. This is preferable, I think, but I find it unlikely, given that the she's lasted this long."

The dim red lighting dyed the water at our feet the color of blood, and reflected in the big, wet eyes of each of my men. They gazed back at me with utter silence, as if they were even forgetting to breath.

Good, I thought. *Better to forget than to be robbed of it.*

I took a step forward and swept my hand through the air in front of me. Even in that simple movement, I felt the moisture and the death clinging to my skin.

"The other way is suffocation. It won't be a quick merciful suffocation, like when you drown and get cut off entirely from the air. No, it will last for ages, and it will be agony. The weaker ones will die first, while the strong count them lucky. You know what tortures they talk of, at the hands of our enemies? Well, not a twisted mind in Germany or Japan could recreate something so terrible."

"Captain!" Perser interrupted. "Stop this! Immediately!"

My eyes sparked, and he knew he crossed a line, but that didn't stop him. "Why are you doing this?" He demanded, "there's still a chance we can survive! If the Royal Navy finds us…or the Americans…"

"Then what, Perser? What?" I shot back. "What means of rescue have we? Even if we are found, those ships wouldn't have the means of saving us. And even if they could get a submarine here, we will have suffocated long before they arrive!"

Perser scowled. "What has happened to you? You have inspired our men with hope throughout this long war. Right, gentlemen?"

If he was expecting a cheer, he didn't get one. They just stared at the pair of us in blank terror. One or two I noticed slipped into sweet unconsciousness in their bunks, the syringes held limply in their hands.

I smiled at the silence. Silence meant death. "Before," I said, quite as the hiss of a leaking valve, "we were fighting a war, men against men. Any man can be outsmarted. Any group out braved. But this—" I tapped the interior hull with my fists. A dull ringing filled the room and was gone. "This is the sea! The ocean! Gravity! Men cannot fight this. They were not meant to."

"Then fight your fear," Perser growled. "For the sake of your men."

"I am doing this for the sake of my men," I said, and pushed passed him. I reached into the satchel once again and began tossing more needles to them. Some caught them eagerly, like treats. Others dodged and stared at them in horror. Some just blinked, letting the thrown syringes hit them like icy drops of rain. It didn't matter either way. They had the choice now. That was the most important thing.

A choice.

Then, Perser's hand closed on my shoulder.

"I can't let you do this," he said. "Those are my supplies. I want them back."

He lunged for them. I held them out of the way, glaring.

"They are my men's supplies. They belong to each of us."

"Oh, *your* men?" He snapped, "the men you are right now trying to kill?"

Behind him, Maloney – who was already injured and in pain from before – slipped a second syringe into his flesh and layed back, smiling.

"I am not trying to kill them," I said. "They kill themselves. Or better yet, the fat, stupid men in charge, sucking cigars in their palace of the sky, kill them. It is not me."

Perser saw my eyes and turned, registering the dying Maloney in horror. He rushed to him, yanking the spent needles from his skin, shaking him by the shoulders.

"No! Maloney, dammit! Hopkins! Jones!" He went from man to man, finding two, three, four, five already dead or unconsciousness. This made me chuckle. In less than a minute, the sweet oblivion of opioids had claimed more casualties than six months at sea had. *How blessed are they?* I thought, *to die so gently.*

Perser turned to me, anger thundering in his eyes. I wondered what he was thinking of. His little girl? His wife? Or the growing weakness of the air; each lungful harder to take and less rewarding.

"How dare you?" He hissed. "Give those to me. Now!"

He lunged again, and I dodged easily aside. He was the medic, after all. Even when we battled, he was not fighting. He was small and twitchy, like a mouse, while I was strong, sturdy, and large. The epitome of British pride. I had seen scenes like this before: the weakling and the bully, the bully holding the weaklings lunch high above his head, while the weakling danced and jumped uselessly. I would be the bully, if I needed to be. What I did not expect, however, was for Perser to throw himself at me, in a full-out tackle.

I slid. The floor was wet, and slimy with oil and grease. My feet flew out from under me and I reeled backward, slamming my head against an outlying pipe and crashing to the floor in a dizzy haze. My hand slipped from the handle of the satchel, and I felt, from a biting breeze on my fingertips, Perser wrench it away. I blinked, struggling to focus, and saw as he raised the pack of precious needles up over his head.

"Mutiny!" I grunted. "Mutiny!"

But he was not angry. He was sad. With a single motion, like a wave crashing upon shore, he brought down the bag with all his strength and slammed it on the metal floor. Then, his upraised foot crashed downward, smashing, grinding, and breaking the fragile syringes into grit. Precious morphine, the one salvation for my men, trickled out in greasy little rainbows mixed with the filth and the flood on the floor until there was nothing left. Watching it disperse somehow steadied my mind, and I rose from the floor like a serpent erupting from the sea.

"How greedy and selfish could you possibly be?" I grunted, and then swung.

If I had not expected his tackle, then Perser had not expected my fist hurdling at him with all the strength of a torpedo. *Boom!* It connected with the side of his face, and he toppled to the floor, as unconscious as the opium-dazed men.

Thomas, our youngest, gasped and gazed in fear, but none of the other men moved. They sat, silent and still, weighed down far too much by the pressure overhead, and by the poisonous air. What was a single fist compared to all that crushing force? I looked at them all, meeting each one still conscious in the eye.

"I will find another way to make our end merciful," I promised. "This I swear to you, on my honor as the captain."

Then I turned and made my way towards the engine room.

****

The hatchway – open for all this long trip – was now sealed shut, emblem to how hopeless things were. These crafts were amazing, and I would always be the first to acknowledge that. They are built to withstand a myriad of emergencies and catastrophes, to be salvageable until they are wholly wrecked. That was our great misfortune: to have been wholly wrecked, and still living and breathing long enough to endure the consequences.

No water trickled in from behind the hatch. My men had done a good job in sealing it closed, thus prolonging their suffering. I put my ear to the metal and could tell there was still water in there. The pressure of it was a silent roar filling my entire being.

Though we feared it, I thought, *you, black rushing death, will be our salvation.*

"Is there any hope at all?" I heard a meek voice mutter from afar. The sound traveled all the way through the sunken boat to scrape upon my ears, for there are no secrets within a submarine. I recognized it as Thomas', and the realization sent a pang through my heart.

I reached down and plucked a wrench from the pile on the floor, near invisible beneath inches of water. It took me four tries to wrap my aching fingers round its shaft, for that's how tired, cold, and dizzy I was. I knew we didn't have long left anyway. Maybe six hours at most. And each one another step into madness, agony, and despair.

"I will open it," I muttered, "And save us all from this hell."

Then, a second voice joined Thomas'. "I don't know, my boy," it said. Perser. Risen. His throat as chapped and raw as arctic lips. Without turning around, I could see the pair of them, huddled close at the officer's table, their jaws drawn and trembling.

I ignored them, and the pain in Perser's voice. Whatever right he had to comfort them he sacrificed when he destroyed the morphine. Even still, I pitied him, and his desperate need to deny the inevitable.

I joined the wrench with one of the bolts in the hatchway and pulled.

The thing screeched like a cat, and white water began to leak out, so fine and thin it was mist. I wrenched again, and the hissing grew, like cold droplets dashed across hot metal.

Perser was speaking. "We could be rescued. Or our mechanics could find a way to start the pumps working. That's the biggest thing, removing the water."

I looked down at the frothing broth at my feet and swallowed a chuckle. Perser had been taken care of. If it soothed him to talk, and soothed Thomas to listen, I was not going to stop them. I had a much greater comfort planned, and it was coming soon.

Another turn of the wrench. Full streams of water now and groaning as the pressure against the hatch shifted. I was surprised my men didn't hear it. They were too busy filling their ears with words, like everybody in this war.

"What of the captain, sir?" Thomas asked hesitantly. "He seems to have lost all hope, and he is such a brave man."

I paused, my hand cold and clammy on the wrench.

"Valence has always been a pragmatist," Perser explained. "When confronted with a challenge, he looks for solutions, not emotions. It has made him brave in this terrible, spiritless war...but I don't think he's felt anything as real as hope for a long time."

A line of water rolled down my cheek. Was it from the loosening bolt? Sweat? A tear? I could not know. It did not matter. I spun the wrench round again, the bolt visibly shifting, and I realized, as the groan rose to a roar, that I was nearing the end. Soon, the door would implode inward, and we all would be swept to sweet merciful death.

Suddenly, it struck me that these were my final moments. Should I inhale, and taste the world one last time?

I tried and realized that there was nothing to taste. The air was thin and bitter, and I could sense the poison in it on the moisture of my tongue. Instead of tasting, I thought to gaze. But that, too, offered nothing. An iron-gray ceiling, black water on the floor; nothing but cramped compartments and mumbled fears.

Nothing pleasant, anywhere. All my senses dulled and pointless, like death.

Nothing to taste. Nothing to smell. Nothing to see. Nothing to feel. Nothing to hear.

Which is why I did not detect Perser creeping up behind me before it was too late.

Crack! My vision erupted in lightning, and my first thought was that it was beautiful. Then, the world swung in a loop as my body crumbled, and I saw Perser standing over me, a long metal bolt in his hands, one of the few we hadn't used to repair the leaks. The tip of it was clotted with blood and some hair, and the brilliant redness of it took my breath away in its beauty.

"You fool, Perser," I muttered. My words felt heavy and distant, and I realized they were slurred. "Now you're all going to die terrible, painful deaths. You should have let me do it."

I expected anger, but instead he knelt down beside me and took my head into his hands as if I were a child. As if I were Thomas.

"When my death comes to me, my friend, it will not be at your hands," he said. The image of his face above me blurred, but whether from his tears or mine, I could not tell.

"You tormentor," I slurred. "You sadist. You cruel man who sits in judgement. Don't you realize what you've done?"

"I preserve hope," he said simply,

"Hope. Hope," I croaked. "There is no more hope."

"There is *always* hope," was his reply.

And so, I had no choice, but to lie there in his arms, with every breath a clawing pain, and every touch a chill, as together we sank further and further into darkness.

Until, at last, it was absolute.

MY BOYS

I couldn't think.

I couldn't think, and I couldn't breathe.

The only thing that kept flashing through my mind was the blood on their bedspreads.

I took the stairs, two by two, and swung myself around every single level of the FBI building before I threw my shoulder into the door. I barreled out into the hallway, stumbled on my feet, and careened my body around the corner. In a quick whirl, I pushed through the glass double doors of the office I had worked at for three solid years.

I could remember the look of surprise flashing through my teammate's eyes as I tried to catch my breath.

"Put them on the screen," I growled.

I watched their eyes widen as they all looked at one another. I wasn't supposed to return to work for another week, and even though my partner had kept me updated on the current case, I technically was not supposed to be working it.

But that bastard had dragged my family into this, and I was officially bringing myself off vacation.

"Put them on the screen!" I roared.

"Laura, just calm—"

"I swear to god, Clarke, if you finish that sentence, you won't have lips to continue flapping."

I was enraged. I was angry, scared, and flailing. I felt my throat closing up on me as my boss, Lawson, stepped forward. His glowering gaze sat hardened on my forehead before I slowly fluttered my eyes up to look at him.

"How did you know more children had been taken?" he asked quietly.

His eyes were begging me…giving me one last chance to open up to them.

One last chance to be part of their family.

"Turn. On. The television," I commanded.

I heard the T.V. turn on and watched the screen slowly come to life. I felt the bile rising to the top of my esophagus as two familiar faces appeared upon the screen. I felt my blood run cold when I saw the slacked, useless jaw hanging from my son's face.

"Aiden…" I whispered.

I clenched my robe closed as my teams' eyes flickered between my face and the television. Their cogs began to turn as they matched cheekbone structure, eye color, hair color, and chin shape. Things only similar between two related individuals.

Things only a mother could pass on to her son.

But then, everyone watched as the camera began to slowly pan out, revealing a second child victim.

I watched as the ebony-skinned young man that appeared on screen, his eyes swollen and bruised with beatings; and my legs began to quake underneath me.

My boys.

This man had both of my boys.

"Oh, no…" I whispered as I stumbled back.

"How old is that boy, Laura?" Clarke asked.

Thaddeus Clarke, my partner for the last three years, worked alongside me from the moment I stepped into the office. He showed me the ropes, traveled with me to crime scenes, and quickly became the brawn to my brains as we scoured dangerous crime scenes and arrested drug/ mob overlords daily.

And now he was looking at me as if he didn't know me, and it broke my heart.

How could I answer his question without divulging the disgusting secrets of my past? How could I admit how old my boys were without giving everything I had run from away?

"Laura," my boss commanded.

It was so hard to breathe, and so very hard to swallow, I couldn't answer him.

"It's obvious you have a son. How old is he, Laura?" he tried again.

"No, Thaddeus…" I choked out. "I don't have a son."

My team furrowed their brows as they took one more look at the television screen.

"I have two," I whispered desperately. "They fit the suspect's motives," I swallowed before I drew in a ragged breath. "All of his victims have been under 18."

"Are those boys under 18, Laura?"

I had never heard my boss's voice that worried before, and it caused me to slowly pan my gaze to look up at his, and the fire behind his eyes slowly died into a low-burning pile of embers.

"They're seventeen, sir," I confirmed.

"But, you're only 32, Culver," Meghan gasped.

Meghan was our residential technological analyst. There wasn't a firewall that could keep her out, or a camera that could obstruct her view. If it was grounded and had a lens, she could get into it. She was of great value to the team, but she also kept herself sheltered from the gruesome content of our cases.

She just...couldn't handle it.

Especially when it involved children.

My eyes slowly met hers as Clarke and Lawson glanced back to the television screen. Clarke crossed his arms tightly across his chest as anger bubbled behind his eyes; and Lawson looked on in utter helplessness.

"You can't work this case," Lawson stated.

"The hell I can't," I argued.

"You're too emotionally compromised," Lawson told me, shaking his head.

"Those are my boys!" I roared as I thrust my finger out at my boss. "I went through hell and back for those boys!"

"Laura, no one is questioning—"

"Zip it, Thaddeus!" I shrieked. "When this was Timothy, did you work the case?" I asked Lawson.

I knew I wasn't being fair. The truth of the matter was the first case I ever worked for the department with this team stemmed around Lawson's child. Timothy had been abducted and taken by a suspect targeting their team, and when the boss screamed for Lawson to be removed from the case, everyone rallied behind him to make sure he stayed.

And I was infuriated that they weren't doing the same for me.

Lawson's shoulders tensed the moment his son's name rolled off my tongue.

"You don't get to be a boss now when the rules of the game got burned to the ground three years ago," I glowered.

Aiden's wail pierced out from the screen as I whipped my head towards the television, and Meghan's eyes grew wide as she slammed her hand back down onto the keys of her laptop.

I watched my son's head get ripped backwards before a darkened hand wrapped around his throat.

I was trembling with anger as I watched the television screen unfold.

"Did you know we had sound!?" Clarke shrieked as Meghan's fingers flew across the keys.

"No…" she breathed as her eyes darted across the laptop screen.

"This suspect only gives us 16 hours to find these children, and we've already wasted one of them bickering over how old I am and whether or not I'm gonna work this case," I spat.

That was when I heard it.

DeShawn's voice.

"Aiden! No!"

He roared for his brother on the screen as I swallowed the vomit down back to my stomach. I couldn't stand there any longer and watch this.

I had to do something.

"I'm going to do this," I continued, "whether or not I have my badge."

"Are you crazy?" Clarke bellowed as he took a step towards me.

"No," I said in a low growl as I shook my head. "But I sure as hell am angry."

Lawson cursed, realizing he had no other choice. The team fought for his right to work the case that targeted his son, and it set a precedence for anyone coming into this team when they did. I remembered back to how eager I was to help, and how I was the only person able to keep a level head because I truly did not know who Timothy was.

Everyone else had been emotionally compromised but me.

And now, the tables were turned: two sons they didn't know were in trouble, and they could work this from the same advantage I had three years ago that saved the life of the boy I now babysat on a regular basis.

"So, what's it gonna be...Lawson?" I snapped. "What's it gonna be?"

****

"Mom!" Aiden yelled as Laura opened the door.

"Ma!" DeShawn called out from the kitchen.

Laura absolutely adored coming home to the sounds of her boys yelling out for her. "I'm home, y'all!" She announced as the boys came barreling down the hallway.

She dropped the three pizzas onto the foyer floor just in time to be run over by two hefty young boys. The house shook with every step they took as Laura giggled and wrapped her strong arms around their necks.

"Mom! You're home!" Aiden yelped as he threw his arms around his mother.

"Hey there, sweetheart," Laura soothed as she rubbed his back. She held both of them close as DeShawn wiggled his arms free and wrapped them around both Laura and his brother, Aiden.

"We're so glad you're home safe, Ma." DeShawn squeezed as her and Aiden began to choke.

"Sweet cheeks. You're killin' us," Laura choked out as Aiden began to laugh.

"Sorry." DeShawn smiled.

"I missed you both so much," Laura said as she cupped their cheeks individually and gave them each a kiss. She ruffled Aiden's hair for good measure, much to his disapproval.

"Mom...come on," he complained.

"As long as you refuse to cut it, I get the right to fluff it." Laura smiled proudly.

"We missed you, Ma," DeShawn admitted before she went in to give him another massive hug around his neck.

"I always miss you boys when I'm gone," she admitted.

She ached whenever she had to leave her boys behind. With this being the start of their senior year of high school, she wanted to make sure she was there for everything. So many things were changing in their lives, and they were beginning to branch out and find their own passions in life. Aiden had gotten accepted into a scholarship program early that would end up paying for two entire years of his culinary education in New York, and DeShawn ended up receiving news that he had gotten a paid internship he had applied for that started the summer before his first year of college.

Doors were opening for the two of them that none of them would have thought possible four years ago, and she wondered what all she would miss every time her boss said she was needed on a case in another state.

The three of them had come a long way from the old days.

"That pizza for us?" Aiden asked, pulling Laura from her thoughts.

"Pepperoni and anchovies for you, ya nasty," she said as she crinkled her nose, "extra cheese for me, and a three-meat pizza for DeShawn."

"Yes!" DeShawn exclaimed as he picked the pizzas off the floor.

"Can we eat on the couches tonight?" Aiden asked.

"Yeah. We could find a good movie on Netflix!" DeShawn smiled brightly.

Laura craned her neck to look up at her sons. Both standing around 6'1", they towered over her 5'6" stature. Her eyes darted between their faces, still seeing the small, fragile boys she had raised rather than the grown men they were slowly evolving into. Tears crested her eyes before she pulled herself back to reality.

"Of course," she whispered. "We can eat out here."

"You alright, Ma?" DeShawn asked.

"Just thinkin'," was all she offered.

"You wanna get the drinks?" Aiden asked as the boys made their way to their respective seats in the television room.

"Only if you find something really good to watch tonight," Laura smiled as she turned to walk into the kitchen.

****

"So, which is it…Lawson?" I asked again, after I'd changed out of robe and PJs I'd arrived at the office in, taking what jeans and shirt Meghan offered me from her locker.

I'll never forget the way my boss looked at me that day. I could see his mind weighing his options as he tried to find some way to snake me out of this. Some way to save my career and my reputation by bucking up and getting me to sit on the sidelines.

But, instead, he sighed and broke the staring contest before he conceded his silent defeat. "Tell us everything," he commanded.

"Not a problem," I breathed.

Everyone began to sit down as my body trembled. I remembered the fears flooding through my mind: how the team would no longer trust me; how my partner would no longer want to be with me; how my boss would find some way to fire me.

I convinced myself I was about to lose my job over this.

I felt my partner's eyes on me even as he sat down at the end of the table.

Getting the farthest away from me that he could.

"Just before I turned 15, I was raped," I began. The entire team fell silent as Clarke locked his eyes onto my face, and my body shivered underneath his intense gaze.

I had never seen him so angry, and yet so hurt.

"When I made the decision to have my son, Aiden, my family was less than thrilled, to say the least. Most people call the situation I was raised in 'high society', and…well…they wanted me to abort. Probably to preserve their image."

"But, obviously you didn't," Meghan stated.

"No. And it got me banished," I admitted.

"They kicked you out?" Lawson asked.

"No. But, I was relegated to a part of the house I grew up in that no one ever went to. Raised Aiden on my own until I turned 18, dropped out of high school during that time and got my GED online because I didn't have any help. When I finally passed all my courses I packed up our things, took Aiden in the middle of the night, and never once looked back." I sniffed hard as all the old emotions rushed back.

"So...who is DeShawn?" Clarke finally asked.

I shifted my gaze to his and held it.

"Did you at least have him willingly?" Clarke spat.

"Watch it," Lawson warned him.

"I did take him in willingly, yes," I said lightly.

"You took him in?" Lawson questioned.

"I adopted him just after I turned 20," I stated.

Clarke shifted in his seat after that admission. My eyes whipped back towards him and his gaze had faltered, falling into his lap as his own past ricocheted off the corners of his mind. I knew it would be a touchy subject for him, what with his own past of being adopted and all.

"You adopted another son at 20," Clarke mumbled.

"Yes..." I trailed off.

My body begged him to look up. The man I leaned on for comfort, trust, and safety in the field for the past three years was dumbfounded as to how I could have kept something to precious a secret from him. We promised each other, from day one, never to lie to one another about anything.

I guess, technically, since he never asked about my family, I never had a chance to lie.

But, to him, not saying anything on my own was a volition that was just as bad.

I had a family, and my best friend didn't even know about it.

"We don't have much time," Lawson stated.

"DeShawn and Aiden were best friends in preschool," I sighed as I closed my eyes. "But, DeShawn's father was…well, not the best."

"Laura," Lawson commanded as I whipped my gaze back to him. "Bullet points," he urged.

"Dad beat him up. Dad went to jail. Family didn't want him. I became family," I stated quickly.

The air grew heavy with my life sprawling out at the drop of a hat. The room hung in silence as it grew with its impregnated truths that bubbled from my lips, but it was DeShawn's voice on the television that ripped me from my thoughts and caused me to whirl back around to the television.

Aiden now had a split and bleeding lip, and was sobbing profusely as DeShawn's voice wafted from the speakers.

"Ma's gonna find us," DeShawn comforted.

I was rooted to the floor as tears slipped down my cheeks.

"Did you know we had audio, Meghan?" Lawson snapped again.

"N-n…no, boss. I, uh…shit…I didn't," Meghan admitted as she began typing along her keypad yet again.

"Ma's gonna find us both," I heard DeShawn whisper.

"Ya damn straight, I am," I whispered at the television screen. "Ya damn straight."

****

Laura sat at her desk as she sipped her second cup of coffee, but she moved too quickly and sloshed some of it onto her shirt. She groaned before she set the mug down onto her desk and quickly rummaged for a napkin of some sort.

"Here," Thaddeus said as he held out a small napkin.

"Thanks, partner." Laura smiled tiredly before she took it from him.

Their hands connected briefly, and Thaddeus gripped his cup a little harder than he normally did.

Today was the day, he had told himself. Today was the day he would finally ask her to have lunch with him.

The two of them always had lunch together, but they always split the bill and she always talked her way into driving.

This time, he wanted to pay. This time, he wanted to drive.

He watched Laura dab at the wet spot on her shirt just before a massive yawn opened her mouth wide, and Thaddeus watched as his partner's eyes watered at the reaction.

"You alright, Culver?" he asked lightly. He cocked his hip upwards to sit on the side of her desk.

"Yeah, Clarke, I'm good," she said through another yawn. "My eyes just water whenever I yawn."

"You not sleepin' well?" He asked.

"I guess I could always use more," she said with a light chuckle.

"Anything I can do to help you out?"

"I don't think so. I swear, nothing's goin' on or anything. I just…have things I'd rather be doing than sleeping, I guess," Laura said as she slowly lifted her eyes towards her partner.

"Sounds like fun," he said and smiled.

"Very." Laura smiled back.

"Could I ask you something?"

"Of course," Laura responded as her brow furrowed.

"It's almost lunch time," he began, "and I figured I could take us around the corner to this little hole-in-the-wall place. I hear it's got a really good burger, and they have those sweet potato fries you always ask for."

"Sure!" Laura said. "Wanna just meet at my car in a bit?"

"Well, I thought maybe I could drive," Thaddeus offered.

That sentiment stopped Laura in her tracks.

"If we made it a longer lunch, I bet we could get a drink at this place, too. My treat," he beamed.

Your boys come first, Laura, she thought; and shied away from what he offered.

"That's really kind of you, Clarke," Laura said gently. "But, I was honestly thinking of just ordering in for lunch. I really don't wanna have to take this paperwork home." She threw in an annoyed grimace, hoping he'd buy it.

Thaddeus felt the confidence draining from his body as the smile he possessed slowly melted from his cheeks.

Burgers and drinks. His partner's favorite indulgent combination.

The plan was practically foolproof.

But the only person that looked like a fool...was him.

"Maybe next time?" Laura asked as she desperately tried to diffuse the tension in the room.

"Of course." Thaddeus nodded before he forced a smile upon his face. "Maybe next week, then."

"Yeah." Laura smiled awkwardly before she dipped her head back down to her desk. Her heart sank for her partner...but she didn't know what else to do.

****

"Here's what we got," Meghan stated. "The suspect has suffered a massive loss in his life. Clarke here saw that it could have been a loss that he didn't fully cope with, surmounting into a massive moment that forever changed his life. We also know," she continued, "that the suspect's taking these kids to places the suspect feels should be important to them."

"Which makes this immensely harder because he doesn't see their life events through their eyes, but through his," Lawson grunted.

"So, he's self-centered," I muttered.

"Not exactly," Clarke butted in. "If he's endured a substantial enough loss and is still reeling from its impact, usually that means he didn't get passed his grieving process."

"How is that helpful?" I spat.

"Each place he takes the kids is a glimpse into his life," Clarke said, his teeth clenched. "If he's taking them to places that are familiar to his past as well as the children's, then he's been scouting them."

"Or somehow had access to that information electronically," Meghan added as her fingertips went back to work.

"Either way, if we can figure out what scenario would most likely have occurred in his life based on the prior places he's taken these kids, we can piece together a bit of his life and run it through search engines to find a suspect without ever knowing what he really looks like," I rattled off.

Everyone whipped their gazes up at me in disbelief.

"I'm still here, y'know," I grumbled lowly to myself.

"Yeah, well, you shouldn't be," Thaddeus uttered quietly, but I still heard it.

"Meghan, work on that theory," Lawson commanded. "Figure out all the plausible scenarios that could be of importance to a person in the venues the prior children were killed in."

"And since we're considering all angles..." I trailed off as I stared at the television. My eyes began to water at the sight of my sons.

"What is it?" Lawson urged.

"What if he's taking them to places that really do mean something to these kids? Maybe...these places hold some sorta...you know, fear to them. I mean...look at them..." My hand lifelessly motioned towards the screen.

"I don't understand," Lawson stated.

"What if they're somewhere they know? You know, a place that holds bad memories for them? I-I-I mean, that man isn't anywhere in this video right now!"

I was grasping at straws and not making any sense, and I knew it.

My hope dwindled with every second lost trying to find those boys.

My boys.

"What if these places don't have anything to do with him at all? What if it really just is all about them? About frightening them to…to try and understand them better?"

"Laura…" Lawson began.

"You think he's trying to better understand his victims *before* he kills them? Thaddeus asked.

"It's a working theory," Lawson breathed before he shot a nasty look towards Clarke.

He was angry. And he had every right to be.

"Found something!" Meghan yelped. "The places the suspect has taken these kids does relate to them! The first one, you know…the abandoned school…it was the school that burned down across town. The sister that was being held there actually lost her older brother in the fire."

My mind finally began to clearly as I urged Meghan to go on.

"And the daycare facility! It shut down for a while because a little girl that was there was given unapproved medication died from an induced seizure caused by lethal mixing."

"Let me guess," Thaddeus chimed in, "the little boy that was killed there was the little girl's brother."

"Yep," Meghan replied.

"What about the third child victim?" Lawson asked impatiently.

"Workin' on it…" Meghan trailed off.

"How did we not know this sooner?" I shrieked as I lost control. "I thought you were the one who was supposed to be lookin' into these connections! It's what you told me!"

I was physically spitting in Clarke's direction, and I was trembling in anger.

This was his oversight.

And it was about to cost me my family.

"Had you fixated on your job instead of trying to slink underneath my clothes, my sons would still be here," I snarled with a glower.

"Maybe if we knew you had sons," Thaddeus countered, "then the FBI could've protected them the moment these victims started popping up!"

"It is not my fault my sons are gone!" I roared before I lunged at my partner.

"Well, keeping secrets during a time like this when they could've been protected didn't help matters!" Thaddeus yelled back as I tried to deck him but missed.

"Be a better agent, Clarke!" I spat.

"Be a better mother, Culver!" Thaddeus jeered back.

Thaddeus spun on his heels and strode out of the room as my jaw slowly unhinged from shock. Tears of anger and helplessness barreled down my cheeks as I whipped back around to the television screen. I heard Aiden howl out in pain just after I watched a blurry figure crack something down onto the side of his head.

"11 hours," a low, growling voice said.

"He's taunting us," Lawson grumbled.

And all I could do was lean up against the wall and sob.

****

"Laura!" Lawson called out. "I'm so glad you could make it."

"I wouldn't miss your cooking for the world." Laura smiled before she hugged her boss around his neck.

"Come on," he beckoned as he ushered her through his front door.

"Culver! You made it!" Meghan cheered. "This is for you."

"Oh, I never turn down a glass of wine," Laura mused.

Thaddeus watched Laura as he stood in the corner. Her long brown hair was thrown up haphazardly in a French twist, and her dangling earrings accentuated the curves of her neck. The gems twinkled against her olive skin, and he watched as her eyes lit up while she talked to everyone in the room.

"Alright," Lawson began. "Everyone ready to assemble a plate?"

"I swear, I do more work here eating food than I do in my own home," Laura teased playfully.

"That's because all you eat is takeout," Meghan chuckled.

"Hey! I can cook a mean macaroni and cheese, mind you," Laura said with a wink.

"You should make it for us one day," Thaddeus commented as he emerged from the shadows.

"Once she can get it from the grocery store," Lawson murmured before shooting a playful look to Laura.

"Jerks. All of you," she said, pointing with her fork.

The food led into popping more bottles of wine open, and soon everyone slowly parted to go their own ways in Lawson's house as Timothy settled down for bed. When Lawson came downstairs from tucking his son in, he turned on some low music to aid in the light conversation for this rare night off.

Laura found herself staring out the window and up at the stars. Thaddeus found his way next to her, looking up at the same set of stars from the same exact window.

"You look wonderful tonight," he said quietly.

"Thanks." Laura smiled kindly.

"You haven't been at the past couple of dinners," Thaddeus recounted. "Wasn't sure if you were gonna be here."

"Well, I didn't have anything standing in my way this time. So, figured I'd show up."

"It's nice to have you here," Thaddeus said before he turned to look at her.

She was painfully aware of how close he was standing. She felt his body heat radiating against her as she lightly sipped her wine. She tried not to pay attention to the inevitable scenario about to unfold, but it was hard when her partner's gaze was so intense.

So purposeful.

So beautiful.

"Can I ask you something?" Thaddeus asked suddenly.

"Of course," Laura said as she turned to him.

"I figured…maybe I'm not being clear with my intentions."

Oh, no. Laura's face dropped slightly at his statement as her grip tightened around her wine glass.

"Clear with…with what intentions?" she stammered.

"Laura…"

He reached out and took his partner's hand. He wrapped his long, strong fingers around her trembling skin, and traced light circles with his thumb on the top of her hand.

It felt so soothing and so sweet.

Her hand blushed red at his touch.

"Will you allow me to take you to dinner?" He asked.

Laura slowly dragged her eyes from their embraced hands and trailed them all the way up to Thaddeus's stare. Meghan and Lawson were staring from across the room, their attention completely on them both, and Laura's breath picked up as her mind raced.

"Thaddeus…I—"

"Before you answer," he interrupted, "let me just say this."

He took Laura's wine glass and set them both down as Laura's eyes watched him intently. He held both of her hands within his, and as his lips moved; she lost herself within the confines of her own swirling mind.

He won't get it.

He wouldn't understand.

He could never accept my life as it is.

She felt her partner's hands trembling with the fear and anxiousness of rejection. She saw his lips hurriedly talking, trying to dig his way out of the personal hell he had created in her in the office. The silent words tumbled from his lips as Laura kept her gaze upon them, and for a fleeting moment she wanted to simply lean in and silence them with her own.

But she couldn't.

Not with her boys.

"Thaddeus," Laura breathed. She knew she was about to do irreparable damage…and yet it didn't stop her from doing it. "I can't."

****

"The only way to know is to re-watch all the tapes."

Meghan looked upon me in horror as Lawson pleaded with his own stern eyes.

"I won't make you do it, Meghan," I reassured her, "but it's the only way we're ever gonna know."

"Know what?" Thaddeus spat as he strode back into the room.

"What we're missing on the tapes because we're distracted with the death of the children," Lawson filled him in. "And we don't have that kind of time," he added.

"If I had someone to go through the tapes with me, I could work on discerning nuanced emotions while someone else watched the background. We'd only have to go through them once, and the person watching the background could technically fast-forward," I stated.

"You can't watch those tapes," Thaddeus piped up.

"And why not?" I bit out before I whipped my gaze towards him.

"Because you'd be watching what's about to happen to your sons!" He growled as if it was obvious.

"I'm working this as any other agent should, and I don't appreciate you talking as if we aren't gonna find my boys," I glowered.

"You think I'm not workin' this case right, Culver?" Thaddeus said.

"I think that's already been proven, Clarke."

"Enough!" Lawson roared. "Enough, the both of ya!"

"I know you hurt, Thaddeus," I began slowly. Tears burned in my eyes once again as I watched him shift his gaze towards mine. "I know you're confused, and you feel betrayed, and you feel like the person you've worked alongside for three years isn't the person that is standing here...in front of you..." I held out my arms as tears ran down my face. "But your anger is with me...not my boys. Don't take that out on my boys," I choked.

And that's when Thaddeus's eyes latched onto mine, looking at me for the first time since that dinner at Lawson's, instead of merely through me.

"Did you think I wouldn't love 'em?" He asked.

But all I could do was stare at him.

"Did you...did you think that, somehow, I would...would *judge* you? For...for the selfless decisions you made in your life? For what *happened* to you?"

I was so scared of answering, so scared of finally pushing my partner to a place he would never return.

A place I couldn't reach him.

"Did you not think I was capable of lo—"

He put his hand over his face and wiped his tears away as Meghan and Lawson looked on in helplessness of a three-year partnership crumbling before their very eyes.

"Did you think I couldn't have loved you. That, somehow, I could have actually loved you because of those circumstances and not…not despite them?"

Thaddeus's voice was a mere whisper at this point… and it broke my heart.

"Do you think you're damaged goods!? Or…or pathetic leftovers!"

I flinched as he threw his hands quickly in the air.

"Clarke…" Lawson warned.

"Did you think I'd see your stretch marks, or loose skin, or whatever the hell it is you hide under those disgustingly baggy clothes day in and day out, and think you were gross? Or even ugly?" He ranted on as if we were alone in the room.

I was shocked at how loud my partner had become. My ears rang and my sternum was vibrating…and yet, he had to say it.

And I was terrified of answering.

Just one word.

One word to tip his world.

"Did you think I would see you the way you see yourself?" He yelled, making me to take a step back as Lawson finally intervened. He stepped in front of me and held his hand out into Clarke's chest, stopping him from coming any further as I backed myself into the wall behind me.

My heart was physically ripping into two.

"Well?" Thaddeus shrieked beyond Lawson's shoulder.

I did the one thing I kept telling myself not to do.

I answered.

"Yes..." I whispered lightly. "Yes...I did."

Thaddeus dropped his arms to his sides and shook his head. He snickered before he turned on his heels to leave the room again, and he made sure to snatch up his coat in the process.

"You comin'?" he hollered. "Thought there were some dead kids you wanted to look at!"

"Jesus, Clarke," Meghan whispered, stunned.

Oh, what a tangled mess I had created.

****

Laura grabbed a pot and wooden spoon from the kitchen before she opened the basement door that led down to DeShawn's room.

"Get up, boys! We gotta full day ahead of us!"

Laura walked down the hallway before she threw Aiden's door open and began yodeling. DeShawn and Aiden yelled at her to hush, and all it did was prompt her to grow louder and louder and louder.

"You got half an hour to get ready!" She sang.

"Mom!" Aiden groaned.

"Get up, big boy!" she called down to DeShawn.

"Food?" he lightly yelled up the steps.

"Always, sweet cheeks!" she yelled back down to him. "Now, boys. Your time starts...now!"

****

Thaddeus sped through the majority of the first few hours of tapes, and I always seemed to stop just shy of the last few minutes. I was watching through every scene of these children dying, looking and listening desperately for absolutely any sign he might have given us that could help. I cranked up the sound system in Meghan's office, determined to keep my ears alert for anything while Thaddeus rip-roared through tapes behind me. I watched, time after time, as a knife seemed to appear out of the darkness and slice open the throats of these beautiful children; it made me so sick I doubled over and vomited into a trash can at my side.

And still, Thaddeus was silent.

I put in the last video without so much as knowing whether Thaddeus had found anything. I sighed and leaned back into my chair as I started the disgusting descent into the most recent child victims.

But suddenly, the tape froze as Thaddeus pulled his hand away from the space bar.

The picture was stilled on the sobbing girl, with her neck craned back and the knife in view. My eyes danced across the screen, they began to widen with what I was looking at.

"What the hell is that?" Clarke breathed.

I pressed a few keys and enlarged the picture in the background, and my skin crawled while I cropped and enhanced the image that hadn't been present in any other video but this one.

It was the outline of a face and a pair of eyes.

Wide, desperate eyes...

I hit the print button and continued to stare at the screen as I registered the desperation dripping from the suspect's stance. His head was slightly cocked, and his eyes were wide and panicked, and it struck me as odd because if someone was killing for pleasure, desperation isn't usually found in their eyes. Enjoyment is.

But this suspect was not enjoying what he was doing. He was…frenzied.

Thaddeus grabbed the piece of paper as I continued to stare at the screen. I listened to him leave the room without so much as acknowledging me while I contemplated the image on the screen in front of my eyes.

Something was off about this picture.

And it bothered me that I didn't know what.

****

"So?" Laura began. "How was it!?"

"Today has been awesome, Mom," Aiden smiled before he stuffed a mouthful of rainbow ice cream into his mouth.

"Who knew Ma liked waterparks?" DeShawn teased before he bit into his chocolate-dipped ice cream cone.

"Did you see her face goin' down that slide?" Aiden laughed.

"Hey, you two wanted me to go down that thing!" Laura giggled before she scooped up some of her banana split.

"You coulda said no!" DeShawn countered.

"Anything for my boys." She smiled at the both of them.

DeShawn returned the grin during the middle of a bite of his cone, and some of the chocolate outside chipped off and landed in Laura's lap.

Laura grinned as she scooped the chocolate off her leg. She eyed Aiden menacingly just before the boy stopped eating his ice cream.

"Don't even..." Aiden warned.

"Don't what, sweet boy?" Laura asked in an innocent tone as she crept the piece of chocolate closer to Aiden's face.

"Don't you dare!" he yelped just before Laura darted her finger out and swiped the melted chocolate across his cheek.

"Gotcha!" Laura shouted playfully.

"Not cool, Mom," Aiden groaned as Laura eyed DeShawn next.

"Uh uh, Ma. Not even," he chuckled.

And Laura leaned over to try and get her other son before he moved out of the way and let her land on the park bench.

"Duped!" He yelled as Laura scrambled to her feet. She left her banana split behind as she chased her son around in the grass, his long legs carrying him far; she had to take shortcuts to get any chance at catching up.

"I'm gonna get you!" Laura yelped as Aiden laughed from the bench seat.

"Try your best, Ma!" DeShawn challenged as he continued to dodge Laura's every move.

"Anything for my boys!" She shouted as she jumped onto his back.

****

Thaddeus burst back into the main office with the paper waving in his hand. He strode over to Lawson and slammed it down in front of him. Lawson bore his eyes into the man's forehead as Meghan asked the question everyone was thinking.

"What's that?" She asked.

"Where's Laura?" Lawson interjected.

"The suspect leaned too far into the camera on the last kill," Thaddeus said as he tapped his finger on the image. "That's his face."

"Where's...Laura?" Lawson enunciated.

Meghan picked up the picture and studied it closely. She committed those eyes to memory before she brushed passed Thaddeus and glared up at him menacingly. "Gonna go get a sketch from this and run it through a database," she explained.

"You're welcome," Thaddeus growled.

"Clarke. Where is Culver?" Lawson raised his voice.

"I don't know!" Thaddeus groaned. "Probably still in Meghan's office sitting like a bump on a log! She practically froze when she saw the face!"

"And you left her there!?" Lawson asked.

"Look," Meghan interjected. "I get it. You're mad because she hid this from you. But Clarke, she hid this from all of us. None of us knew she had kids."

"You mean none of you knew?" Thaddeus exclaimed. "Even Lawson, who has to approve her health insurance paperwork?"

He wheeled around to his boss who now had his chest puffed out. He was getting tired of Thaddeus' attitude, and he was about to toss him from the case.

"I don't do that anymore. Haven't for a while now," Lawson reasoned.

"None of us knew she had kids?" Thaddeus shrieked.

"Thaddy," Meghan said trying to calm him down.

He whipped around to face her with anger bubbling behind his eyes. He bent his torso towards her, towering over her small frame before she stepped out from under him and clenched her teeth. "You're being selfish," she murmured.

"Self...selfish?" He stammered. "I'm being selfish."

"Yes," Meghan stated. "Laura just sat here and gave us a quick rundown of her entire life, and you weren't even listening! Clarke, she was raped. And she kept the child! And her parents disowned her. Then, she adopted an abused child out of the goodness of her heart before she could legally drink, and now? Now, her sons...the two things she cherishes the most in the world...are..." She looked at her watch before she blinked back tears of her own. "They are 9 hours away from being killed," she choked out.

"And you're so preoccupied with your own broken heart that you aren't even stopping to consider why she did it in the first place," Lawson picked up for her.

"She tell you why?" Thaddeus asked, the edge in his voice fading away.

"No. But, you do remember the first case she ever worked with us, right?"

Realization slowly spread across Thaddeus' face as everyone focused wholly on his revelation. "Timothy..."

"Laura came in for that interview mere moments before I was informed that my son had been taken. Before she was even hired, she offered her services to help, and that is the only reason Timothy is still alive and breathing...because she was the only one not emotionally compromised within that case."

"Coming into something like that as a mom…" Meghan said "… especially with everything she's been through? Can you blame her? Really, truly blame her for any of this?"

Thaddeus put his face in his hands before Lawson let out a heavy sigh.

"She kept them a secret to keep them safe," Lawson said lowly.

And that was it. That was when Thaddeus's mind began churning.

"Say that again," he said slowly.

"Say what?" Lawson asked.

"'She kept them a secret to keep them safe.' That's what you said!" Thaddeus exclaimed.

"Oh, no…" Lawson murmured.

"What?" Meghan asked.

"That's what you said!" Thaddeus yelped before he turned on his heels and barreled out of the room.

"What?" Meghan yelled.

"She kept them a secret from us. And if she can do that for three years…" Lawson trailed off.

"Oh, god. Our suspect knows her," Meghan gasped.

Thaddeus sprinted down the hallway towards Meghan's office. He crashed through the doors as his legs burned, begging for Laura to be there when he finally came to his senses.

But all he saw was an empty seat and a mugshot that was pulled up onto the screen.

Thaddeus ran to the chair and sat down to look at the face on the screen, but when he sat down onto the padded surface he yelped in pain before shooting back up. His eyes trailed to the computer screen once again before his blood ran cold, and his heart fluttered in fear for Laura's life.

"Clarke!" Lawson boomed before he appeared in the doorway. "She down there?"

"No," Thaddeus murmured before he held up Laura's badge and gun. "We have a problem."

****

"High, Mommy! High!"

Laura pushed Aiden higher in the swing as DeShawn grasped her pant leg tightly. He shook, his small little form pressing itself deeper into her calf as his eyes darted around.

Laura sank down and took his shoulders before her eyes met his watery gaze.

"What's goin' on, sweetheart?" She asked lightly before she brushed his tears away from his bruised cheek. DeShawn didn't answer.

"You know it's alright to talk to me, okay? I'm not gonna hurt you," Laura promised while she held the frightened boy's gaze.

"Th-th…thank you…foh-w…taking m-me…to the…th-th…the pawk," DeShawn hiccuped.

"Sweet cheeks, if you don't want to be here, we can always go home. Or, we could go see a movie, or maybe get some food?" She choked back her own tears at the sight of the frightened boy as Aiden's swing wound down.

"Wuh-s wrong, Mommy?" Aiden called out as he planted his feet back onto the ground.

"I don't know, baby boy," Laura said before she wrapped her arm around him.

"What do you want to do?" She asked DeShawn. His teary gaze panned back up to hers as he struggled to catch his breath, and all she could do was embrace him and pull him close so as to shield him from the harshness of the world.

"Can I...call you 'Mommy'...like, uh...like he does?" The trembling boy asked.

Laura's lip trembled against the little boy's shoulder, and as Aiden slipped his arm around DeShawn and pulled him even closer, she held both of her sons in the middle of the playground before a small smile spread across her cheeks.

"You can call me whatever you want," she assured him.

"Ma?" DeShawn asked before he peeled away and looked up at her.

"Yes, sweet cheeks?" Laura asked, wiping the tears from her face.

"Can we go get fwench fwies?" DeShawn asked.

"Oh, you want some fries, huh?" Laura smirked. "I think we can manage some fries," she smiled.

And both of her boys took her hands as they walked back to the car.

****

I raced down the highway and careened off an exit before I switched the black SUV's flashing lights off. I took a sharp left-hand turn onto a darkened town street, and I continued buzzing down the road as it brought me into a dilapidated town.

It only took me moments of staring at that face to figure out why those eyes seemed so off.

They were familiar.

I pushed the speed limits while I continued to weave my way through the small town, and as the sides of the roads gave way to older, crumbling homes, I knew I was headed in the right direction. House after house passed with peeling side panels and foundations crooked with termite damage. I kept my eyes wide for pedestrians as I kicked up the speed on the car.

I had made this drive far too many times to ever forget it.

My fingers gripped the steering wheel hard as my mind whirled back to the shaded picture of that man's face while he swiped that knife against that poor girl's neck.

Those eyes.

Those desperately familiar eyes.

I had looked at those eyes every day for the past 14 years.

I turned down the last road before I cut the lights off on the vehicle completely, and slowly inched the SUV closer, and closer to the house I knew he was keeping my boys in.

Right at the end of this dark road.

It was the house DeShawn was born into, and it was the hellhole I plucked him from when he turned four.

A shiver ricocheted up my spine as the words of my own mouth echoed off the hallways of my mind.

"... the suspect takes them somewhere that pertains to pain."

How could I not have seen this sooner?

That man had been released.

That man had my children.

I put the SUV in park in the crooked driveway before I completely cut the engine, and sat, listening to the chirping crickets outside as the silence of the night slowly dawned upon my ears.

There was no going back now.

I opened the car door and made my way to the rear doors. I threw them open before I grabbed a crowbar I had stashed in the back. I sighed, flipping it in my hand, when another thought dawned on me.

The reason why I had grabbed a recording device.

If I was going to alter the course of my life forever, I had to make sure they were taken care of.

I had to make sure my boys would be alright.

I picked it up and made sure it had a tape in it before I hit the blaring red record button. I drew in a deep breath.

"I, Laura Culver, being of sound mind and body, do hereby give full and complete guidance and medical decisions of my two sons, Aiden Culver and DeShawn Culver, over to my partner, Thaddeus Clarke of the FBI. My estate, passed down to me by my parents, Angel Culver and Dale Culver, that totals more than $50 million dollars, with no other siblings to claim property, is to be split equally between my two sons once they reach the age of 18. Until such time, Thaddeus Clarke of the FBI oversees all decisions regarding the estate, under the assumption that any decision made shall have the input of my sons, no matter the age."

Tears filled my eyes before I clicked the recorder off, and I set it in the middle of the back, leaving it wide open for the team to find. Continuing as planned, I clenched down onto the cool metal in the palm of my right hand.

My eyes slowly meandered up to the front door of the dilapidated house, and I noticed it hanging wide open.

That door wasn't open when I had first pulled into the driveway.

"Ring around the rosie…" I began to quietly sing as I approached the opening of the doorway.

****

"… pocketful of posies!" the boys called out as the twirled around in the backyard.

"Ashes! Ashes! We all fall DOOOOOOOWN!"

They plopped into the muddied mess of the backyard from a massive spring rain, and Laura watched them with a smile on her face as she washed dishes at the sink. Her 7-year old boys were having a ball in the puddles in the backyard, and she knew she'd have to shoo them into a bath before they sat down to eat dinner. Laura giggled and shook her head before she continued to scrub the dishes at the sink.

"Wait until I tell them what that song's about," she murmured to herself.

The doorbell rang out, and she looked up once more to check her boys before going to answer. Their voices were ringing out loudly, and if she heard them giggling, her nerves abated.

"Ring around the rooooooosie!" they began again.

She wiped her hands onto her pants before she opened the door and took stock of the FedEx man standing there, holding out a slim envelope.

"Just need a signature, ma'am," he said and smiled kindly.

Laura's eyes widened before her fingers signed a shaky signature, and she took the envelope from the man's hands, ripping the cardboard wide open.

It was here.

It had finally arrived.

She bid the FedEx man a half-hearted goodbye before she closed the door and ran back to the kitchen, and just after she raised her eyes to see what her boys were doing one last time, she pulled the paper from the cardboard envelope and to scan the words.

Two years.

It had taken them two years to get to this point.

Her eyes dripped with anxiousness and her lip quivered with fear before her eyes took in the printed words, and those tears of anxiousness turned to tears of joy as she read the first paragraph over, and over, and over again.

"In accordance with the adoption laws of Washington, D.C., I am extremely pleased to inform you that the Council has approved your application for adoption for one (1) DeShawn Miller Sullivan."

Laura sank to her knees in the middle of her kitchen as she listened to the growing sound of her boys singing loudly in the backyard.

"Ashes! Ashes! We all fall DOOOOOOOWN!"

****

Lawson raced down the highway as Thaddeus leaned heavily into the car door. Meghan was typing away furiously at her desk in her office, and it was what she said in their inner ear that confirmed Thaddeus' fear.

"We're headed in the right direction, I can hear her voice on the camera feed on the television."

"ETA?" Thaddeus asked Lawson.

Lawson's hands were white-knuckling the steering wheel just before the SUV careened towards an exit on the highway. "Still 10 minutes out."

"Even at this speed!?" Thaddeus shrieked.

"Don't worry, Clarke," Lawson soothed. "We'll get to 'em."

"How could she not have known he was out?" Thaddeus snapped. "He should've been a top suspect the moment those boys went missing!"

"That's enough!" Lawson roared as he took a sharp left turn. "You've ridden her enough. Meghan and I have to support her, stand back while we do the rest. Because right now, you're not helping."

He shot Thaddeus a glowering, predatory look before he sighed heavily and sank back into his seat. They navigated down the darkened roads filled with abandoned homes, when Meghan piped up into their coms once again.

"We know you're heartbroken, Clarke," she began, "but she did this all for a good reason. She was trying to protect her kids, and, in return, she kept you from dating her because she felt she was damaged beyond repair. In her mind, she was saving you from someone because she felt you deserved better."

"She thinks she's too damaged?" Thaddeus asked.

"Isn't that obvious?" Lawson shot back.

"You guys should be pulling up to the house. It's at the end of the road you're on," Meghan informed them tensely.

As they hit the drive, they saw the parked SUV in the driveway of an old, run-down home, and Thaddeus' eyes widened as he threw his door open upon hearing a piercing sound ricochet through the nighttime sky.

"Ma! Please! No!"

****

I slowly stepped into the house with the crowbar swinging at my side before I closed the front door behind me. I gave my eyes time to adjust to the darkness of the rank-smelling home while the tape of my boys played in my mind. I filtered through the pictures, searching for any visual clues on the tape as to where they could possibly be in this house.

But to me, the only room that made sense was DeShawn's nursery.

I slowly walked through the house with the floorboards creaking underneath my feet, when I heard a thunderous crack and DeShawn crying out into the night.

"Dad! No!" He roared.

I picked up my pace and swung my body around the banister of the stairs, taking them two by two before I yelled into the house. "Get your hands off my son!" I jumped into DeShawn's nursery; the crowbar swinging high above my head, but I soon realized it was unnecessary.

The room was completely empty.

I backed out before I continued down the hallway and heard the faint whimpers of my son as my heart clenched in my chest. Tears brewed in my eyes, and my pleading soul called out involuntarily to the son I couldn't see but was desperate to rescue.

"I'm coming for you, big boy!" I roared through the darkened home.

"Ma! Help!" I heard him cry back out to me.

The sounds, they weren't coming from up here.

They were coming from below me.

I scaled the stairs and strode my way towards the basement door, spotting the light trail of blood. Dried and cracked, it led down the cement basement stairs, and my anger bubbled inside of me, and fluttered underneath my skin.

In a moment of clarity, I knew the reality of my existence.

I was going to kill this man.

Slowly, I descended the stairs before I heard the light muffled sounds of who I thought was Aiden, and as I breached the corner to the left, a shiver shot down my spine, and an anger like no other flooded my veins.

Aiden was bound to a chair with his dislocated jaw hanging haphazardly from his face, and DeShawn had his left eye swollen shut with his nose and lips bloodied. They were both moaning in agony, struggling against their restraints.

"Wh-wh-...who's there?" DeShawn cried out. His voice- trembling with fear- broke my heart as my tears flowed down my cheeks.

"It's me, big boy," I soothed, my eyes darting around the darkened basement. "It's just me."

Aiden groaned in pain again, and vomit rose through my throat before I swallowed it back down.

"Where are you, you blatant coward?" I yelled into the room.

At this point, I knew Meghan could probably hear me on the tape, and I didn't care what she witnessed.

"What? You think I didn't know you were out of prison? Alive, well, and settling back down into the area!?" I roared. "You think I wouldn't keep tabs on my son's nightmare?" I spat viciously.

"He's not your son," a voice rose from the darkness. I watched as both of my boys winced at the sound; and I grasped the crowbar tighter in my hand.

"Well, he most certainly isn't yours," I snapped.

"You took him from me," the man growled.

"Like he took your wife from you?"

I knew that was the issue. Once I realized who he was, I knew the issue that was fueling him: I knew that he blamed DeShawn for the death of his wife.

Dying in childbirth, however, is never the infant's fault. But not to this man.

"I've forgiven my son for his...indiscretions," the man leered.

I finally saw the outline of his body emerge behind my boys, it shook me to my core as I tried to keep my voice steady. "You really do blame him, don't you? A 7 lb. 9 oz. infant for the death of your wife. Roger, she chose to carry him to term. She chose—"

"You know nothing about my wife!" He roared.

I watched as he shifted around the boys before his tall, broad form appeared quickly in front of me. "I know she knew about her cancer!" I shrieked. I cocked my crowbar back and whipped it around, smiling when I heard it connect with his stomach. "I know she chose to carry him to term instead of abort him and seek treatment!" I roared before I cocked my leg back and kicked him in his face. "I know that she loved you!" I yelped before I brought the crowbar down hard onto his back. "And I know that she loved DeShawn!"

I grasped the crowbar with both of my hands before I slowly raised it over my head.

"And I know that she trusted you with his life."

I was ready. I was ready to feel this man's blood trickle underneath the heels of my boots. I was ready to smell the iron that would waft from his body as he bled to death at my toes, and the animalistic instinct within my body blurred my vision as my motherly instinct cried out for vengeance.

I was going to kill this man.

But, it was DeShawn's shrieking cry that pierced through my muddled mind and penetrated down into the darkest, deepest, most vengeful depths of my riled being.

"Ma! Please! No!"

****

Thaddeus opened his car door while Lawson was still in the process of slowing the vehicle down, and the man unlocked his seat belt before jumping out and barreling towards the house. Lawson parked and ripped the keys out of the ignition before stumbling his way out, finding himself beside his colleague before his phone vibrated.

"Talk to me, Meghan," Lawson demanded.

He drew his weapon as Thaddeus stared at the open door. He knew what was about to happen, the desperation pouring from his partner. He knew he had to stop her from making a very grave mistake.

"FBI!" Thaddeus roared into the home.

"Yes, got it. Thanks, Meghan," Lawson said before he hung up his phone.

Thaddeus quickly drew his gun before whipping his head around to his boss. "Well? What did she say?"

"She thinks they're in the basement," Lawson said.

The two of them slowly made their way into the house as they cleared every corner. One by one, rooms were marked clean and safe as they made their way down the hall, and it wasn't until they rounded a corner that they saw a door hanging wide open. Lawson slowly reached his hand out and peeled the door back before he yelled down the steps.

"FBI!"

Thaddeus rushed through the door and descended the stairs, and Lawson had his gun trained on the empty space as they both cleared the wall. Their hearts were pounding in their ears as they tried to mentally process this entire scenario. It wasn't until the wall broke and they saw me poised above the man, ready to bash his head in with the crowbar, that Thaddeus made a split-second decision.

****

Thaddeus raised his gun towards me.

"Ma!" DeShawn shrieked as his father groaned at my feet.

"Ma...don't be like him," DeShawn begged.

All the words…words of comfort and of love…words of devotion and reassurance…they were all replaced with spit-fire words of fury and fear as my mind raced. The metal of the crowbar felt so freeing in the palms of my hands, and the reality of why I was truly angry slowly dawned upon me.

"He took you two…from your beds…" I growled.

He had come into our home and violated everything that was supposed to be safe about it. A bed was where you allowed your vulnerable and weak body the rest it needed to recuperate. A bed was where you were weakest.

And he had violated that.

"Laura?" Thaddeus said firmly.

I slowly turned my head over to the staircase to see my partner with his gun trained right onto me, a disgusting laugh peeled from my throat.

"Really, Clarke? You hate me so much you're willing to kill me over him?" I asked.

"I don't hate you," Thaddeus breathed before he shook his head. Lawson stayed in the shadows with his gun trained on the forehead of DeShawn's father, just in case he decided to make a move against any one of his teammates.

Or my sons.

"Save your heroic speech for someone who cares," I choked out before I turned my head back to the man at my feet.

"I won't let you kill him," Thaddeus said as he took another step towards me.

"But you were willing to let him kill my sons, right?" I asked before I whipped my head back towards Thaddeus. "You were willing to place your tender, broken heart in front of the well-being of my boys.

Right? You were willing to place your selfish, hurt little feelings in front of figuring out how to save my sons' lives, right!?" I bellowed.

The sound caused Aiden to groan in pain as he tried desperately to peel his eyes open.

"And now?" I shrieked before I turned my entire body towards Thaddeus.

My partner.

"Now you're willing to shoot me instead of the serial killer who has ripped apart seven different families! All in the name of trying to get his back?"

At my weakest and most vulnerable moment, DeShawn's father made a move towards me. He flew up faster than I assumed possible for a man his size and hit me in my stomach as I fell to my knees, gasping for air. DeShawn yelled in the background and Aiden tried desperately to free his hands to get to me. DeShawn's father brought his large hand down onto the back of my neck and bashed my head into the concrete floor.

Multiple gunshots rang out while my body collapsed to the floor, and warm, thick trails of blood were now seeping up against my aching body. My eyes flickered over towards the source, and I was met with a pair of lifeless eyes. The man, his eyes wide open and his jaw unhinged, stared wildly at me, almost as if he was still accusing me for taking his son.

Staring into those eyes, I finally grasped the gravity of the situation.

Murderer.

I had almost become a murderer.

I scurried to my feet as the room spun, and I made my way over to my sons. I untied their legs before Lawson approached them from behind and freed their arms. It wasn't until someone turned on a light that realization dawned upon my mind.

DeShawn couldn't see his father like that.

I ripped the last of Aiden's bonds away before I stood up quickly, and as I prepared to throw my body into my son's line of sight, my eyes took in my partner as he fluttered a blanket over the dead, bleeding body.

"I've got it," he said comfortingly as his eyes glistened before he hastily wiped at them.

The paramedics traipsed down the stairs minutes later and the tears streamed from my widened eyes before I turned back around and helped Aiden into the arms of the people there to help. The medics worked an IV and some pain medication into my son's arm while some attempted to clock and chart all of the pain and suffering that had been inflicted upon him.

My son.

My little baby boy.

"Ma…" DeShawn croaked.

I whipped my head around and dipped quickly at my waist before I took his face in my hands. I planted a long, deep kiss upon his forehead as paramedics swarmed the trembling boy, and tears dropped into his lap from my face before I whispered into his skin.

"Hey there, sweet cheeks."

"Ma…" he croaked again. He threw his weakened arms around me as I pulled him close, slowly rocking him side-to-side. Just as I had done so many times when he was a child.

"My big, sweet boy," I whispered as I held him.

I pressed another kiss to the side of his forehead as the blood of my son soaked into the fabric of my shirt, and just when I thought I was going to lose my composure, a hand came down on my shoulder.

"The medics are here for him," Thaddeus told me gently.

"He kept insisting, Ma..." DeShawn choked out.

"Who kept insisting what, sweet cheeks?" I breathed before Lawson appeared behind my son. He dipped into my line of sight before he put his hand on DeShawn's back, hoping that, in some feeble attempt, he could quell the trembling of the large boy who was being shielded by his mother.

"A-... Aiden," he said, sniffing.

I furrowed my brow and pulled back to look my son in the face. I took my finger and crooked it up underneath his chin, lifting his swollen, bruised, and bloodied face up to mine.

"He kept insisting what?" I asked lightly.

"To hurt him. He... he kept telling my... my dad—"

"That man is not your dad," I said sternly. "Your father, yes. But most *certainly* not your dad."

DeShawn peeled open his good eye and flickered it up to me. I stood in front of him as the paramedics moved in on his broken form, and Lawson helped get him up from the chair, so they set an IV into his arm.

"Ma?" He asked before he felt the pinch. "Ma?" He asked a bit louder as they moved him to his gurney.

"I'm right here," I soothed as I reached out for my son's hand. My tears dripped down the length of my neck as the fear in my son's eyes etched lines into his face. "I'm right here, and I'm following the two of you to the hospital," I whispered.

"You can ride with us, Mom, if you want," the paramedic smiled as they wheeled DeShawn to the stairs.

"Please, Ma…" DeShawn begged.

"Alright, baby boy. Alright," I said before I turned my head to look back towards my boss.

And all he did was nod.

Everyone emerged from the house as they watched me hop into the ambulance. The doors shut with a slam before the lights and sounds struck up their familiar symphony of agony, and just before Thaddeus went to hop into the SUV to follow the ambulance, Lawson ripped him over to the vehicle I had driven to get here. But then they were out of sight and all I cared about were my sons.

****

"What, boss?" Thaddeus asked with wild eyes as he hurried to Lawson.

"You need to listen to this," he urged.

Thaddeus looked down at the recording device with confusion painted all over his face. He glanced back up at his boss with a quizzical look before taking the recorder from him, and just before he went to go press play, he sucked in a deep breath.

"What is this?" Thaddeus asked warily.

"A lot of things," Lawson began. "But mostly? It's how she feels about you."

That was enough for Thaddeus.

He jammed the play button down on the device, and the crackling of the leaves in the background slowly gave way to a familiar voice as he latched onto every single word his partner was saying.

"I, Laura Culver, being of sound mind and body, do hereby give full and complete guidance and medical decisions of my two sons, Aiden Culver and DeShawn Culver, over to Thaddeus Clarke of the FBI..."

<u>MUtANt</u>

A large gust of wind surged in every single direction, and a mound of papers fluttered to the floor. Agent Lori Conwell sighed when she saw the last folder sitting on her desk; and she couldn't help but groan at this new, and frankly reckless, ruling from Congress.

As mutants became more accepted into society- with their powers, and superhuman strengths- the government was beginning to see their uses in other facets of the American people's lives. Jobs would include: super-soldiers, black ops forces, intelligence agencies, and all of them were contracting out while utilizing mutant humans with specific talents to aid them in their jobs.

Now, Congress had ruled that every single team in every single intelligence department was now required to have a full-time, hired mutant on their staff.

A knock sounding at the door ripped Conwell from her thoughts. One of her team members opened it a crack and peered in at her.

"Knock knock," R.J. teased.

"Come on in, R.J.," Conwell beckoned.

"No luck with the speedster?" she asked, stepping inside.

But all Conwell did was continue to stare at the last folder, forever distracted until she could let her fingers reached out and flip the file open.

"Can you send in the last applicant?" Conwell breathed deeply in, and out through her nose, trying to keep her patience.

"No one's out here, boss." R.J. furrowed her brow. "You sure you called everyone?"

"I know I did," Conwell snapped.

Then, just as Conwell went to reach for her phone to dial the last home phone number, a body appeared behind R.J.

"Agent Conwell," the strange individual lulled lowly.

R.J. jumped, her hand flying to her chest as she raked her eyes over the form of the person standing beside her; shocked at the stranger's surprisingly normal state.

"Katie?" Conwell asked before she stood to her feet and smoothed out her shirt.

Katie's eyes slowly drifted to the desk as she studied the wide-open file sitting upon the dark, bare desktop of Conwell's office.

"Come on in. Sit down," Conwell beckoned.

Katie slowly stepped into the office as R.J. stepped off to the side. She gingerly made her way to the chair in front of Conwell's desk, while she kept her eyes locked onto the Agent. Conwell found herself clearing her throat before turning her attention back to the file.

"It says here you can... fly?" Conwell asked.

But all Katie did was blink at her.

"And... 'manipulate elements'?"

"Is that an interview question?" Katie murmured before she quirked an eyebrow.

"Should it be?" Conwell shot back.

Katie's face didn't change. Conwell's attitude didn't faze her, and she found that oddly pleasing.

"It says here you also... create telepathic links," Conwell stated.

"Funny," Katie began. "It also states I graduated top of my class, have a Doctorate in Psychology, five years of experience with the local D.C. police force, and have top honors in all of my physical and tactical examinations."

Conwell slowly panned her gaze to Katie, whose deadpanned eyes were locked wholly on the Agent's form. Katie was analyzing her, and she didn't like that.

"I suppose none of that is really important, however, given that I'm the last mutant application you have to interview before you choose someone," Katie deduced.

Conwell couldn't help but be impressed… even though she was backed into a corner. She didn't like corners. She closed her file before she tossed it to the side, and sat down, sighing lightly to herself.

"You're very qualified for this job," Conwell began.

"But you can't risk the safety of the team you personally chose, and built to someone who you fear is reckless," Katie prompted.

Conwell was utterly surprised at the fact that Katie could have come to that conclusion. "Are you reading my mind right now?"

And, for the first time, Katie smirked. "No. I create telepathic links. I am not a telepath."

"There's a difference?" Conwell shot back.

"Your ignorance is astounding," Katie replied, sounding bored.

"Would I know if you were reading my mind?" Conwell asked, curious.

"Yes," Katie stated.

"How?"

Katie shrugged one shoulder as she said, "It tingles."

A hard knock came at the door, and both women whipped their heads towards the sound. Conwell beckoned entry, and an older gentleman with a nicely-trimmed goatee, and a thick Italian accent stood in the doorway.

"Got a case, Conwell. Three different victims in ten hours."

Conwell nodded before she stood from her seat and held out her hand towards the stranger; Katie took the cue and rose.

"Gio. This is our mutant recruit, Katie Holmstead," Conwell introduced.

"David Giordano," he said with a bob of his head. "Welcome to the team."

It didn't surprise Katie that Conwell had hired her: she was left with no other option, with no other applicants to speak of, and being forced to comply with the law.

"David Giordano," Katie smirked lightly as she held out her hand, "pleasure to meet you." Gio stared at her hand before Katie cleared her throat. "I don't bite. Not one of my things."

Her words earned a hearty chuckle from Gio before he reached out and shook her hand. Katie held his grip for a moment, then scooted by him and headed for the conference room. Gio looked after her as Conwell stood beside him, and it was Conwell who broke the silence.

"We need her for the team to be in regulation, otherwise we can't operate. If anything, hiring her will buy me more time to find a more suitable team member."

"You don't think she's suitable?" Gio asked.

"I think she's intentionally closed off, and on a team like ours we have to be able to trust one another at the drop of a hat," Conwell stated.

"Well, then let's drop this particular hat, and see what happens before we write her off completely," Gio said with a wink.

Conwell shook her head as the two headed into the conference room, and they saw Katie standing off in a corner while the rest of the team sat around the briefing table.

"Everyone," Conwell began, "this is Katie Holmstead. She's our new recruit, so make sure she feels welcome."

Everyone craned their heads back and acknowledged Katie, and some of them even smiled lightly towards her. A few studied her more than others while the rest got their heads back into the file in front of them. One of the men got out of his seat and came directly over to her.

"Dr. Sean Scott," he said as he held out his hand.

Katie shook it and locked her gaze with his as she intently stared at him. Her eyes raked up and down his form before her hand began to lightly pulsate with electricity, and Katie furrowed her brows lightly before Sean dropped his hand and released hers.

"Alright, you guys," a bubbly, stringy man said as he bounded to the front of the room. "Take a seat and let's get this puppy rollin'. Welcome, Katie. I'm Maxwell Hernandez, the chief resident expert in all things technological," the bubbly persona said by way of introduction.

"And colorful, I see," Katie smiled.

"Always, sugar," he said with a wink.

"Now," Hernandez began, "three bodies, all found in this area: the Appalachian Trail in the mountains of North Carolina."

Katie watched the presentation screen as a map popped up with a shaded circular area superimposed on top, and she finally dropped her gaze to the file in her hand as her eyes took in the four mauled bodies paper-clipped into the folder's flap.

"Looks like an animal got to 'em." R.J. grimaced.

"The only thing connecting them is their gender: male. I've done some preliminary searches, and besides the obvious differences in physical features, none of them frequent the same areas... or even live in the same cities," Hernandez rattled off.

"Not true," Katie murmured from the corner.

Everyone slowly turned their chairs and heads towards her as her gaze slowly panned up to Hernandez.

"They're all mutants."

"How do you know that?" Sean asked.

"A mutant knows when it's in contact with another one," Katie stated while she shifted her gaze to him.

"Even from a simple picture?" he asked.

"Yep," Katie said shortly.

"Alright. Male and mutant," Hernandez sighed, pinching the bridge of his nose. "That means they're in the database somewhere, and we can figure out what they did. You know, power-wise."

"Hernandez, keep on that," Conwell commanded. "Everyone else? We're in the air in 20."

Katie finally broke her stare on Sean's face and she closed her file with a thud. She watched as everyone quickly filed out of the room, and just before she went to go push herself from the wall, R.J. appeared at her side. Katie stared at her as she lightly shifted from foot to foot, and patiently waited for her to say something. Then, an idea crossed her mind.

"What's your favorite flower?" Katie asked.

"What?" she asked confused as she snapped out of her trance.

"Flower. Favorite. Go," Katie said pointedly.

"Well... I guess—"

"Water lilies," Sean chimed in as he appeared out of nowhere. "Water lilies are a good one if you can't think of one."

"Alright." R.J. smiled brightly. "A water lily, then."

Katie smoothed her long black hair off her shoulders and turned her gaze away from them as she exposed her neck. Then, as if prompted by nothing other than magic, a pulsating motion ricocheted underneath her skin near her pulse point before a flower slowly grew from under the flesh. It slowly emerged from the side of her neck, blossoming before their very eyes as the soft petals laid themselves out along Katie's skin.

"Take it," Katie beckoned.

R.J.'s trembling hand reached out and plucked the beautiful flower from the crook of Katie's neck. Sean smiled brightly at Katie when she turned her head back towards them, and R.J. stared at the flower in awe.

"See you on the plane," Katie said as if nothing odd just happened, well at least not for her. She sidestepped them silently to get to the door.

****

The plane ride was quiet. Everyone was studying the case file while Katie looked outside to watch the clouds pass by, fascinated with how they wrapped around the wing of the plane. Her heart beckoned to spread her arms and soar out there among them; taking in their beauty while basking in the heat of the sun. However, she settled for hunkering down in the closed-off metal cabin with a team that didn't want her there, and a boss that wouldn't care if she fell off the planet into a boiling vat of lava.

Suddenly, a loud plop in the seat in front of her tugged her from her thoughts of soaring through the clouds, causing her to sigh, and close her eyes.

"I know you wanna be left alone, so I'll make this quick," R.J. said.

Katie didn't say a word, which prompted her to continue.

"I don't want this team getting hurt. The flower trick was cool, but you're a risk. Mutants have been known to be higher targets and putting them in the field places everyone around them at risk."

Katie nodded lightly in response.

"Especially if it's the type of harm that outmatches their ability to escape," R.J. said lowly.

Katie knew what she was getting at.

"If you're holding something back, you have to tell us. About this case, or about you," R.J. stated.

"I'm not gonna hurt your team," Katie murmured.

"I'm not talkin' about you... at the moment, at least." R.J. slapped her folder down in front of her before she jammed her finger into the images. "I'm talking about what you saw earlier that we weren't able to see."

"It's all just theories at this point," Katie mused before she placed her forehead against the tiny window. She just wanted to push out and be free...

"That's what we do here, Katie. Theories based on facts."

"And I have theories based on nothing," Katie countered as she slowly panned her gaze to the woman in front of her.

"Then, let's bounce some ideas off each other," R.J. offered.

As Katie's eyes settled harshly onto R.J., she watched as the woman shifted in her seat. She glanced around the airplane, and saw the entire team looking at her through side-glances before they, too, shifted uneasily.

They were terrified of her.

Every single one of them.

Even Sean… and that was the most perplexing of all.

"Not with you," Katie finally said.

"Then find *someone*," R.J. muttered as she got up out of her seat and made her way towards the back of the plane.

Katie knew she was right. Even though she wanted to continue living in her peaceful, comforting world, away from all the judgmental glances and the harsh realities her life afforded her, R.J. was right. Someone else needed to be working these theories with her, if for no other reason than to keep this team safe.

"Scott," Katie called out.

Sean stopped his conversation midway through his statement before his gaze found hers.

"Come here for a sec," Katie beckoned.

He looked tentatively at Conwell before he got out of his seat, and Katie listened as his footsteps falling heavily behind her head. Sean appeared in front of her and studied her closely before he took the seat where R.J. had been, and cleared his throat.

"What's up, Katie?" he asked.

"It's been… brought to my attention," Katie began, "that my theories, though not technically rooted in facts, should still be shared with someone else on the team."

"Sounds like good advice. Want me to get Conwell?"

"Figured I'd share it with someone who could help me keep them safe," Katie said lowly before her eyes flickered up to his. "You know… if my theories turn out to be right."

"Wh-wh-... what uh... makes... makes you think I can help with that?" Sean stuttered.

Katie closed her eyes and sighed heavily before her gaze whipped open hooking onto Sean's. *I won't tell them,* Katie whispered into his mind as Sean's eyes widened profusely. *Calm down. Just... calm down, Sean. They don't know, and they don't suspect,* she reassured him inwardly. The two of them stared at one another for quite some time, even with knowing the team was eavesdropping onto their conversation. Katie leaned back into her seat before she pinched the bridge of her nose to keep herself on track.

"These three men in the file are mutants. I know just by looking at their pictures. A mutant spotting another mutant, is like a mother knowing the gender of her child before the big reveal: it's an intense, overwhelming sensation, and to call them anything else feels innately... wrong."

Katie studied Sean as he slowly settled into his seat.

He looked almost... comfortable.

You promise? Sean replied through the link between their minds.

Katie lightly nodded her head at his silent question. "But, these aren't animal wounds," she said aloud, getting back to why she needed him over here. "Animal wounds are always centered around massive muscle groups: thighs, the back, sometimes the forearms. The *meat* of their kill, quite literally. These markings, however, are all in opposite locations: the stomach, love handles, their cheeks. Places where close to no quick nourishment would stem from when it comes to an animal."

Sean blinked a few times, appearing amazed by her conclusion. "So... what're you saying? You think a person is doing this?"

"Not just a person... but a mutant. And, I think I know which mutant it is," Katie told him firmly.

"And when were you going to divulge this information?" Conwell snapped. She hovered over Katie's shoulder while staring intensely at Sean, and Katie could tell it was making him uneasy.

Settle down, Katie urged.

"When we got to the station after landing, and the Police Captain told you that there was someone already in custody, and willing to talk to us," Katie explained.

"You mean… the mutant you believe is doing this is currently on his way to the police station?" Conwell asked hotly.

"Willingly?" Sean piped up.

"No," Katie stated matter-of-factly.

As everyone on the plane fell silent, hanging onto her every word, Katie's eyebrow slowly quirked up into the air as she simply said, "*Her* way."

****

When the team finally got to North Carolina, none of them bothered checking into their hotel first. They simply grabbed their travel bags, and headed straight for the police station. Mostly because this case was high-profile, and because the team wanted to see if Katie was right.

Conwell and the Captain found one another quickly before slinking off into a corner to talk, and everyone else piled into the room that looked on into the interrogation room. The wild woods-woman was handcuffed to the table, and none of them could believe their eyes.

It looked as if Katie was right.

"How did she do that?" R.J. murmured.

Sean shrugged, too in awe to speak.

"Doesn't look like she went quietly," Gio murmured to R.J. as everyone clocked the leaves in her hair, and the massive scratch across her cheek.

But Katie just chuckled to herself before her phone rang on her hip.

"Katie speaking," she said lightly as she answered it, her tone of voice startling every single person in the room with her.

"Hello, my luscious new agent!" Hernandez crooned over the phone. "I *finally* got into the mutant database. Might I add, it was housed behind more firewalls and protocol than our own Pentagon, and I figured out the powers our former mutants possessed."

"Hit me," Katie said as a slow smile ricocheted across her cheeks. She pulled out a sharpie from her pocket and rolled up the sleeve of her shirt to begin writing.

"Alright," Hernandez began. "David Morris had some serious strength. Kyle Johnston had something called 'chameleon abilities', and Tyrone Davis was a jumper."

"Of buildings or through other parts of the world?" Katie asked for specification.

For the first time in the team's history, Hernandez fell silent over the phone.

"Hernandez. The distinction is important," Katie implored.

"Of buildings," Hernandez informed after a bit of typing on his end.

"Great. Thanks," Katie said.

"So cool!" Hernandez squealed into her ear, and Katie chuckled… which shocked the team even more. She stuffed her phone back into her pocket before the door opened, and she gazed up to Conwell as the boss walked in and stood beside her.

"I think it's gonna be you who will interrogate her," Conwell informed her shortly.

Katie drew in a deep breath through her nose, and she rolled her sleeve back down, when a familiar voice shocked her from behind.

"Maybe I should go in with her," Sean stated.

"Not until we know what's going on," Conwell threw back.

"But Holmstead can keep me safe, right?" Sean asked, his gaze flickering over to Katie.

What are you doing?" Katie asked tightly.

Sean shrugged off her silent question, and his gaze hardened onto his boss. "You're never gonna be able to trust her until you see that she's on our side," he stressed.

"And you trust her?" Conwell asked, stepping in between Katie and Sean.

"We've always been the type of team to trust until we have concrete proof that we can't. If anything, her being a mutant on this team makes her the most trustworthy one out of all of us because she possesses the most ability to protect us," Sean postulated.

"And she can turn on us on a dime," Conwell murmured lowly.

"So can any of us on each other," Sean shot back.

Katie watched the debacle emerge, and she was beginning to realize why Sean acted the way he did… why he *hid* the way he did… and everything was slowly beginning to make sense.

"I'm going in with her," Sean stated firmly.

"Scott—" Conwell attempted to interrupt.

But Sean had already grabbed Katie's hand and pulled her from the room, slamming the door behind them as they stood in the hallway.

"And while we're in there," Sean called out from the hallway, "you might wanna ask yourself if you really *are* as unbiased as you say you are."

Katie's eyes widened in shock as she stared at Sean's face. Her head cocked to the side, and Sean's hand maneuvered them in front of the door to the interrogation room; she paused before placing her hand on the doorknob.

"You sure?" Katie murmured lowly. "Because this could… become revealing."

Sean knew what she meant, but his hesitation barely lasted a second. He nodded, and Katie took a deep breath to calm her own mind while her gut churned with nervous energy. She didn't know where this was headed, but she knew it wasn't going to be good.

For either her or Sean.

Finally, she found her strength, and twisted the doorknob quickly. She threw the door open into the room and allowing her eyes to descend on the haphazard woman in front of her.

"Hello, Claire," Katie greeted her with a smile on her face.

****

"Angel!" Claire exclaimed as she leapt to her feet. Claire broke the cuffs as if they were made of streamers and threw her arms around Katie's neck. "My god," she gasped. "How long has it been!?"

"Seven years." Katie said with a smile while she pulled back from the hug. "This is my partner, Agent Sean Scott," she introduced before Sean held out his hand.

Don't say anything about it, she added silently to Claire.

Claire gave a subtle nod as she said, "Agent Scott, it's very nice to meet you."

"Likewise." Sean nodded.

Katie could tell Sean was happy to be in common company, and she was thankful for his ever-present confidence, but she knew he must have been shaking in his shoes with the entire team watching the interaction. If Conwell was as perceptive as she lead them believe, no doubt she had already figured out what Sean was.

"You know the drill," Katie stated, leaning back into her chair.

Sean leaned forward onto his forearms before he drew a deep breath through his nose. "State your name, place of residence, and abilities," he rattled off.

"Claire Brahms; Banner Elk, North Carolina; taking other's abilities," Claire stated.

"Wait," R.J. said aloud on the other side of the glass. "Her ability... is to take other's abilities."

"Would appear so," Gio muttered, puffing his cheeks out in exasperation.

Sean's eyes were wholly locked in fascination onto Claire as Conwell stepped to the front and pressed her nose to the glass. Then, everyone watched as Claire's face slightly faltered.

"Claire...?" Katie questioned, urging her to continue.

"The way I garner their powers," she began, "I have to bite into them. Well... technically... I have to drink a certain amount of their blood."

"She's a mutant vampire." R.J. cursed as she shook her head.

"Where do you typically bite people?" Katie asked.

"Angel, do I need a lawyer?" Claire asked instead of answering.

"Why is she calling her 'Angel'?" Gio wondered aloud.

"I believe I can answer that question," Conwell said roughly, holding up her phone that housed Hernandez's face.

"You guys! Listen, alright. Guess what?" he chattered.

"What's up?" Gio asked thickly.

"I thought Katie looked familiar, so I did some digging around in this mutant database. Awesome stuff, by the way. Turns out her file is under complete lock and key; encrypted, parts of it redacted, its own firewalls... everything."

"Why do I feel a classic 'but' coming on?" R.J. smirked.

"But," Hernandez exclaimed, "I opened her file long enough to take a screenshot before it triggered an alarm."

"An alarm?" Conwell snapped, glowering at him.

"Don't worry, boss lady. Got it all figured out," Hernandez promised.

Conwell opened her mouth to lecture him when everyone's phones dinged.

"Katie Holmstead's case file name is 'Angel'," Hernandez stated.

"Case file name?" R.J. questioned.

"Back about three decades ago, there was a mutant registered in the system who was born to two non-mutant parents. It said her parents were offered a great deal of money to turn their child over to the government for testing. You know, to try and figure out how a mutant child could be born to two people with non-mutant DNA," Hernandez explained.

"I take it that's not the true story?" Conwell asked.

"Not if you call her parents being found dead, four days later on the side of the road fishy instead of circumstantial," Hernandez said with an angry grunt.

"Leave it to the government," Gio spat.

"But that's not all. She's not just the only mutant born to a non-mutant couple. She's also categorically the strongest. Apparently, the mutant community literally knows her as 'Guardian Angel'."

"Thanks Hernandez," Conwell stated.

"Anytime!" he chirped before cutting the call.

Gio chewed on the inside of his cheek, watching Conwell closely, seeing the gears turning in her mind before he stated, "You think she's emotionally compromised."

"Isn't she?" Conwell moved closer to the window, watching closely.

"Honestly?" R.J. butted in. "I think you're more compromised than she is."

Everyone turned their gaze back to the interrogation room as Conwell stared wide-eyed at her team. No one else said a word, and R.J. merely shrugged.

"Looks like they're still talking about a lawyer…"

"Not if you're innocent," Katie repeated for the third time amidst Claire's scared ramblings of not wanting to talk anymore. "That's why I need you to be honest with me before we start looking at things. I need you to tell me where you were last night between the hours of 11 PM and 3 AM." The room was silent for a solid ten seconds until Claire hung her head, and Katie's stomach dropped when recognition wafted over her face. "Before you say what I think you're gonna say," she said gently as she stretched her hand out for the other woman's, "just answer one question."

"Alright," Claire whispered with tears in her eyes.

Is there any way to transfer the powers you acquire to someone else? Katie breathed into the minds of both Sean and Claire.

Sean whipped his head over to look at Katie while her eyes stayed wholly connected with Claire's. Tears slipped down Claire's cheeks before she turned her hand upwards, embracing Katie's in a loving clasp as their fingers intertwined.

All they've been needing is the blood, Claire breathed back, and out loud she said very seriously, "I would like a lawyer, please."

Katie finally released Claire's hand, sighing and leaning back into her chair as Conwell came barreling through the interrogation door.

"You two, with me," Conwell beckoned harshly.

Katie and Sean rose to their feet before Katie cast another glance behind her. Her heart ached for her friend, and she knew something wasn't right. Claire was being used somehow. The interrogation room door shut with a thud before Conwell turned sharply on her heels.

"Lawyers are usually something we attempt to avoid," she said pointedly as her eyes fell onto Katie. "However, asking for one is usually a good indication of guiltiness on some level."

"Yes," Katie stated plainly.

"I'll have her charged, and arrested within the hour," Conwell spoke before she began to turn her back.

"No," Katie stated plainly again.

Conwell slowly turned around as Sean stepped up to defend your position.

"I get that you don't trust her," he said loudly, "but, you trust me, right? And *I* trust her. You don't know the whole story of what just went on in there." He pointed behind him for emphasis.

Katie side-glanced Sean, trying to warn him with her eyes that he was toeing on very delicate ground right now between staying in the dark, and being forced into the light.

"Then would someone like to fill me in on what exactly I just saw?" Conwell asked, crossing her arms and glaring at them both.

"First off," Katie said, "I get it. You don't trust mutants, and I can work with that. What I won't tolerate is you laying blame where blame isn't necessary. While I wholeheartedly believe that Claire is the one doing this to these men, I can guarantee you that she isn't doing it maliciously, and is probably being coerced."

"Coerced?" Conwell asked. "Explain, now."

Katie found it very convenient that she had sidestepped the accusation thrown her way… and in that moment, she realized why Sean was staying in the dark. And it made her furious.

"There are rumors in the mutant community," Katie said, took a breath to keep herself as calm as possible, and continued. "Rumors of an organization attempting to synthesize abilities to be able to sell on the black market to ordinary people."

"What's it supposed to do? Give them powers?" Sean asked.

"Temporarily. The serum, once injected, can last anywhere from two hours to two days, depending on the concentration of the dose."

"Which probably affects the price," R.J. stated as she stepped up to the group.

"I would assume," Katie agreed.

"So, then why not just kidnap the mutants, and keep them hostage?" Sean postulated. "Why kill them just for one serving of blood?"

"This is where we get into the genetics of mutants that I'm not familiar with," Katie admitted.

"Well, there are many theories," Gio said, taking over as his body approached the rest of the group. "The widely accepted one is that mutants can only create the chemical in their system that gives them their powers for so long at such an exponential level before it gives out altogether."

"Like an overworked organ," Katie stated.

"Like… mutant diabetes?" Conwell asked. Her hands slowly dropped to her sides, and it didn't go unnoticed by the team.

"You could think of it like that, yeah," Sean said.

"So… what? These dead men we found are mutants that can't harness their powers any longer?" R.J. asked.

"And how does Claire fit into all of this?" Gio asked. "I mean, is she the one supplying them with mutants to take? Or, is she the one keeping them hostage, and supplying them with the blood?"

"Neither…" Katie trailed off as her mind whirled. She brought her hands up to her face to rub her eyes, trying to stave off the sleep trying to barrel her to the ground. "I think they have her on retainer," she murmured.

"What do you mean?" Conwell asked. The edge in her voice was finally gone, and it caused Katie to slowly look over at her.

"I mean, I think she's the one that figures out whether or not their tapped out," Katie stated as her eyebrows hiked up onto her forehead.

"That would make sense," Sean butted in. "If she bit them and she didn't acquire their powers, it would mean they didn't have any more to be taken."

"So... what now?" R.J. asked. "Where do we go from here?"

Gio smiled as he looked down at his phone before revealing to them a conversation he had been having with Hernandez while they were all postulating theories. "We do what we always do," he said before he handed the phone to Conwell. "We follow the money."

****

When Claire's lawyer finally arrived, it came as no surprise to Katie that the lawyer was also a mutant. The search team Conwell sent out headed to Claire's home, and a couple of hours later they found themselves back at the police station with a staggering amount of evidence bags.

"Sean?" Katie asked as he walked up to her.

"There's absolutely no doubt that those bodies, and many others, were in her home. Even if she is just an accomplice to something bigger... even if she is being bribed or held against her will... her deal is still gonna come with jail time," he emphasized.

Katie felt like she was about to vomit.

"Any luck with the money trail?" R.J. said as she made her way to stand on her other side.

"Yeah. Leads back to an empty trail of shell corporations. Never the same one, and never the same face to the account on the other end," Katie sighed annoyed.

"I take it the account numbers are always different, too?" Sean asked.

"Yep," Katie snapped. "Yep they are."

"Holmstead," Conwell called from across the room.

Katie sighed before she made her way around the desks, and Conwell dragged her off to the side before she began to talk lowly.

"We have to find a way to get Claire to talk. We have all these loose ends, but absolutely no way to tie them into anything."

"One thing we need to do is start working on her plea deal," Katie stated.

"Plea deal?" Conwell repeated with an arched brow.

"Jesus… Conwell, didn't you work in law at one point?" Katie shot back.

She was right. Before Conwell had taken on this team she had been one of the most prominent prosecutors in the entire D.C. area. "I just don't understand—"

"She's a mutant!" Katie raised her voice to interrupt her boss. "Not a species from another planet! At her base, she is human. Just like you!"

Katie's tone drew everyone's attention, watching as her eyes began to change from brown to gray.

"If she were a regular human woman in this situation, what would you give her to entice her to talk?" Katie asked desperately as Conwell's hair blew back from her ears.

There was a massive surge of wind wafting from between Katie's lips, and it had Conwell rooted to the ground in shock with everyone in the station watching Katie intently as her hair slowly changed to silver, starting at the roots.

"Get the woman a deal to make her talk, like all the other criminals with information you want access to," Katie growled.

She closed her eyes, and took deep breaths trying frantically to control the emotions raging within her. She couldn't allow herself to get out of control, not in a closed room full of people.

It would only prove Conwell right, in the end.

"And stop being so damned prejudiced," Katie murmured before she turned to walk away. She ignored the eyes that followed her, and she rounded a corner into a dark room before she backed herself into the darkest corner available and crouched down.

"Breathe, Angel," she whispered to herself as she finally felt the calming relief flood her body. "Breathe…" she said before she exhaled the last cool, spiraling puff of air from between her lips.

"So… when your file says 'elements,' you're talkin' more Captain Planet, aren't you?" Gio's thick Italian voice wafted from the door of the room.

Katie was forced to shake her head and flutter her eyes open. "Sure, as hell ain't the periodic table."

"I'm sure Sean won't be too disappointed." Gio smiled.

"Why would Sean be disappointed?" Katie asked confused.

"You don't know? Sean has multiple doctorates, but one of them is in Physics."

The silence that wafted between Katie and Gio was almost… soothing to her, in a way.

"We all need sleep," Katie broke the silence, unsure of what else to say.

"Yep. I came to find you to let you know that Conwell is releasing everyone to go check into the hotel. Finally."

"What about the plea deal?" Katie asked before she stood to her feet.

"Nothing will happen until tomorrow. But, until then? Claire's gotta go into a holding cell for the night."

"No. You can't put her there. Besides it never holding her, if we're talkin' about some super-secret powerful organization, who's to say they won't get to her, and kill her?" Katie asked worried.

"That sounds a bit unbelievable," Gio said with a nervous chuckle.

"This entire situation is unbelievable," Katie emphasized.

She walked closer towards Gio as he stepped out of the way. She could tell he was contemplating her statement, and she crossed her arms over her chest before leaning up against the frame of the door.

"Come on," he said while he held out his arm for Katie to take. "I think I have a solution to our issues."

****

"Protective detail?" Conwell quirked.

"Well, yeah. Send Claire home and have Angel accompany her for the night until the plea deal can be discussed, and handled tomorrow," Gio stated.

"My name's Katie," she murmured.

"Well, we aren't just sending her, and I'm not sending one of my agents alone with her to do this," Conwell argued.

"Why do you hate us so much?" Katie asked as she whipped her head up to look at her boss. "Why do you automatically assume I'm working up some kind of devious plan to...to undermine your authority, or kill your team!?" Her fists clenched at her sides, and her insides churned uncontrollably as she stared hard at her boss.

"Because that's the only interaction I've ever had with a mutant!" Conwell said sternly.

"No, it isn't," Sean chimed in as he walked into the room.

"Sean..." Katie warned.

"No, no. It's alright. I promise," Sean said as he put his hand on Katie's shoulder.

"Scott?" Conwell eyed him heavily.

And then, right before everyone's eyes, Sean pulled out a knife and held up his arm. Everyone watched intently as the blade came closer to his skin, and Gio reached out, and grabbed his wrist carefully before the older man's eyes raised to plead with the young boy genius.

"It's alright, David," Sean said lightly.

Apparently, Katie wasn't the only one who knew, judging by the look in Gio's eyes, a fatherly worry of what was about to happen. Everyone gathered around to watch as Conwell's eyes widened, and Sean raked the blade across his skin, peeling back the cellular layers as blood pooled to the surface. When he was done, the blood sucked back into his skin and the wound closed quickly... right before everyone's eyes.

Katie couldn't peel her eyes away from him.

"Oh, my god," R.J. murmured.

"Shit…" Katie whispered to herself.

"This whole time?" Conwell asked lightly as she raised her gaze to the young man.

"I'm sorry," Sean said with a shrug. "I just… I was gonna tell you guys, but then things happened with Barber, and this was before it was mandatory to list this type of thing on employment applications… and things just spiraled, and I…" He trailed off, licking his lips nervously, unsure of what else to say.

To Katie, Sean was no longer the tall, thin, strong individual she met her first day with the team. His eyes now betrayed the lost boy inside of him. The one hiding from a team he loved dearly.

Katie's stare was rooted on Sean's face while he looked pleadingly towards his boss.

"Laura… I'm so sorry," he breathed.

"Who's Barber?" Katie asked quietly.

Conwell raked her hands down her face and sighed heavily. Her shoulders slumped, her eyebrows furrowed, and her body gave way into the wall while she pressed the heels of her hands into her eyes. "Holmstead, take Sean with you on your protective detail," she ordered.

"And me," Gio added.

"Whatever," Conwell sighed as she shook her head, and turned her back.

Katie had never seen a woman more tired, and more defeated than the shell of a woman standing in front of her. She watched as R.J. rounded the group and went to go lay a loving and tender hand on her boss's back.

"You still haven't answered my question," Katie prodded before she turned her eyes to Sean and Gio. "Whose Barber?" she asked while they exited the room.

"Maybe later," Gio said lightly.

They gathered Claire, and all went out to the black SUV. The car bobbed and weaved down the dark, wooden-thatched road, until the bright lights finally landed upon a smooth pathway that broke out into a driveway for a cabin.

"This is it," Claire told them.

Gio pulled the car up to the house, shut the engine down, and before Sean could throw his door open, his hand reached over, and his gun-roughened skin came down onto Sean's wrist.

"Are you alright?" he asked lowly.

"I'm more frustrated," Sean admitted.

"At what?" Gio asked.

"At the fact that revealing myself didn't change the way Conwell acted towards Katie, but it did change the way she acted towards me."

"You can't really fault her for that," Gio said as everyone climbed out of the car. "I mean, look at the experience she had with Barber."

"I take it this 'Barber' character was a mutant?" Katie asked as her and Claire rounded to the front of the vehicle.

"Yeah…" Sean trailed off.

"What did he or she do that was so bad?" Katie breathed.

"He killed Conwell's wife," Sean informed her.

Katie felt like swallowing her own tongue. "Well still," she said quietly as she composed herself. "Just because I've had shit luck with men doesn't mean I hate all men."

"What, uh... what kind of luck?" Sean stuttered.

"Scott." Gio chuckled as he shook his head. "Not quite the same, Holmstead," he shot back as they all watched Claire unlock the front door.

"Fine. A better example: just because 'regular' men killed my parents doesn't mean I hate, and are apprehensive around all regular men," she said instead.

Both Gio and Sean whipped their heads around to look at her as Claire shoved her shoulder into the front door.

"Come on in," Claire muttered.

"Telepathic, remember?" Katie tapped the side of her head. "I knew from the moment they were planning it what was about to happen to my parents. Don't see me holding Conwell hostage for their sins, do you?" She murmured before shoving past the two men on the porch, and following Claire inside. As Gio and Sean stood in shock on the porch, they both turned their gazes towards one another before they both heaved a deep sigh.

"Slightly better example," Gio murmured.

"I'll say," Sean sighed, and hung his head for it was going to be a long night.

****

"What if they come after me?" Claire asked while her hands trembled around a hot cup of tea.

"Then we'll be here to stop them," Sean reassured her while he ran his hand comfortingly up, and down Claire's arm. "You said it yourself: the men that come are just regular men."

"That doesn't make sense, though," Gio said, frowning. "I mean, you're obviously much more... everything... than them. Why not just—"

"Kill them?" Claire bit out.

"Thanks, Gio," Katie sighed from the fireside.

"I mean, it's an option," Gio murmured.

"He's trying to figure out what is keeping you from retaliating against them when they are the ones that come to you. Do they have something they're leveraging against you?" Sean asked.

Katie hadn't thought about that option. She turned her head, and studied Claire and Sean closely. Her back sunk into the warmed wall beside the fireplace as she watched Sean's eyes dance around Claire's helpless face, and her breathing became silent as she hung onto every word she knew Claire was about to spew. Katie slowed her breathing, and closed her eyes, mentally standing at the precipice of Claire's swirling mind as dates, numbers, and voices slipped inside of her own. She knew she couldn't jump into Claire's mind, but the thoughts whirling at the forefront gave her enough to know what was going on.

"You tried to stop them, didn't you?" Katie said quietly.

Claire slowly shifted her gaze over to the sound of Katie's voice. "Yes," she whispered.

"How did they originally sell this to you?" Katie asked as she set her elbows on her knees. "What caused you to believe you were helping?"

"Katie, I think that's—"

"Scott, three men are dead. She might be a mutant, but we treat her no differently than if she were a regular person dumping bodies that a secret organization no longer needed for their experiments."

Katie could tell her words cut Claire deep, and it calloused her soul to know she was inflicting this onto her friend. But she had to know her motivation behind all this. What was in it for her? Katie knew Sean's newfound sense of "home" would cloud his judgment, and it was why she was so glad Gio insisted he come along, because all he was doing was nodding in agreement.

"She's right."

Katie's eyes slipped over to Sean, and she studied him. Really took a look at him. The fact of his doctorate degrees rolled around in the back of her mind as she observed his prominent jawline, and his frazzled hair that hung just above his ears. She moved to his pillow lips, and his twinkling gaze that held nothing but a childlike awe and worry for Claire's circumstance. She wondered at his ability to be the foundational rock for this woman whose life had been ricocheted into a corner that frightened her… that so many mutants had found themselves in; and none had ever escaped from.

He was an enigma, and Katie found her mind reaching out to his as her breathing slowed, and her brain focused.

She couldn't stop it. It was as if something drew her to the edges of his skull. She closed her eyes, and opened them, finding herself at the precipice of Sean's mind as calculations, theories, numbers, voices, and formulas whizzed by Katie's head. It was unlike anything she had ever witnessed: chunks of memories, impossible equations, and paragraphs of dissertations running through his head all at once. In all the minds she had ever probed, she had never witnessed anything like it.

Thank you, Katie breathed into his mind, and it caused him to jump before he whipped his gaze over towards her.

"Makes you feel violated for a second, doesn't it?" Claire chuckled.

The comment caused a little moment of laughter between everyone in the room, and Claire cleared her throat.

"They were claiming to be able to get rid of powers," Claire finally spoke up.

That got everyone's attention.

"There are mutants all around us that have wished all their lives that they never had them. Mutants that have prayed day in, and day out that they would one day wake up, and whatever God or...or evolutionary force of nature would just take from them what it so selfishly gave."

"So, these men told you they were making something to get rid of them?" Gio asked, to be clear as he crossed his leg over his knee.

"Yeah. But they said it had to be person-specific. They needed DNA, and marrow samples from the mutant to reverse-engineer a compound for a serum that would then negate the effects of the chemical in their body producing their abilities."

"These men we found. They were all men who wanted their powers gone?" Katie questioned.

The flickering of the fireplace cast sharp shadows on her furrowed brow as Sean's gaze locked heavily with her face.

"Yeah..." Claire whispered before tears sprang to her eyes.

"How did they spin your job to you?" Katie prodded.

"Angel, I—"

"Claire," Katie interrupted. "You have got to fill in the blanks. They're working on a deal for you right now. You're getting that. But, now you have to help us."

Claire cried, bringing her hands up to her face, and weeping into her palms. Sean rubbed her back, and Gio got up to kneel in front of her. A sudden pang of jealousy rushed through Katie's veins at the sight, and she shifted uncomfortably, trying to get it to go away. No one ever attended to her like that when she was helpless and crying.

"They promised me a free engineered serum for myself if I didn't ask questions," she sobbed.

They used Claire's own disgust for herself against her, Katie realized, and her hands curled into fists on her thighs. An overwhelming fury coursed through her veins as her hair turned silver once again.

****

When Katie finally calmed down, she was breathing deeply with Sean rubbing her back while murmuring lowly in her ear.

"Hey. It's alright. You've more than proven yourself on this team. Without you, we would never have made this type of progress. Especially on the first night. Just take a deep breath…"

His low voice tingled the back of her neck, and his palm on her back felt so… soothing. She never felt at peace like this, and it caused her to physically have to choke back her own tears, so she focused on what was in front of her.

Claire.

Beaten and broken down, facing jail time.

Katie puffed the last of the cool air from between her lips and fluttered the pages of the magazines on the table in front of her. Sean drew in a deep breath through his nose.

"You alright?" he asked.

"I will be when we catch these asshats," Katie growled furiously.

The light chuckle that reverberated from Sean's lips caused Katie to smile slightly, until Claire's voice sounded on her other side.

"Here," she beckoned, handing Katie a steaming cup of apple cider.

"Bless you," Katie moaned as she felt the warmth of the mug cascade up her arms. She sipped the warm beverage, smiling at the warmth trickling down her throat, and filling her stomach; soothing her even more.

"What is that, by the way?" Sean asked. "You know, when you change like that."

"Angel here can control the elements," Claire said as she wiggled her eyebrows.

"Like the periodic table!?" Sean exclaimed.

It caused both Gio and Katie to stifle a laugh.

You were right," Katie breathed into Gio's mind. Startlingly enough, it didn't seem to bother him like it did everyone else. He simply looked down at her and winked.

"No," Claire said. "Like fire. Water. Earth. Things like that."

"Water, wind, light, fire, earth, and electricity," Katie added.

"So, that's how you grew the flower?" Sean asked.

"Oh, it's so much cooler than that," Claire murmured.

"Must be if it impresses another mutant," Sean said in awe as he hiked his eyebrows up onto his forehead. "Why did you turn gray again? Like you did at the station?"

"Each element has a color. Depending on the element I'm wielding, my physical features take on those characteristics."

"Like… red hair with fire?" Sean asked.

"Mhm," Katie hummed before she took a sip of her cider.

"Or… blue with water?" Gio asked.

"Yep," Katie replied.

"So, gray is…?"

"Wind," Claire answered for her.

"Are they hooked to your emotions somehow? Because you've been very upset when it's happened," Sean observed.

"Not really. They aren't triggered by emotions all the time, just the stronger times I feel them. But, they can also raise their heads of their own volition if I don't keep a handle on them, and if a certain color decides to make an appearance, it triggers the emotional state it is connected to." Katie explained.

"Emotions aren't always the cause, but always a byproduct. Got it." Sean nodded as if he just understood some crazy equation he'd been working on.

Katie couldn't do anything but smirk at him. She watched as his mind tried to make sense of it all. She slowed her breathing once again and closed her eyes. She teetered on the edge of Sean's mind yet again, and she was astounded by the equations and information he tried to fill in. He was talking to himself at a rate that was hard for Katie to even process, and it was as if his mind was a constant whirling vortex of information, and processes.

"She's done that twice now," Claire murmured to Gio.

"What is she doing?" he asked.

"Standing at the tip of his mind and looking in. Think of it as standing on a cliff, and looking out at the sunset," Claire said with a soft smile. "The water doesn't know you're there until you jump in, but you can still see the top layer of the water without immersing yourself in it."

"She's literally standing at the edge of Sean's mind?" Gio asked on a breath.

"Yep." Claire smiled. *Like what you see?* She breathed into Katie's mind.

It caused her to jump and pull back from Sean's mind before her neck began to flush in embarrassment. But, before Sean could ask what caused her to jump, everyone heard the cracking of twigs, and leaves off in the distance.

"Shit," Gio spat.

"That's them. Oh god, it's them. Th-th-... they're here!" Claire whispered harshly.

"Here, come with me," Sean beckoned, reaching for Claire's hand.

But then, an idea struck Katie.

"Claire," she stated before she sat her cup down and got up from her chair. "You said you wanted to stop them, right?"

"Well, yeah," Claire nodded.

"What if I told you I think I have a way to get you out of jail time?" Katie smirked.

She could hear the vehicle getting closer, and closer to the house; so close that the lights of their car began to shine in through the windows of Claire's home.

"Oh, no. Absolutely not, Holmstead," Gio argued.

"It's not your choice," Katie countered.

"What's...what's the idea?" Claire asked.

As Katie's hands slowly encompassed Claire's head, she brought the frightened woman's forehead to lean on hers before Katie fluttered her eyes open.

"Telepathic link," Katie whispered lightly.

****

"You let them what?" Conwell roared. She was no longer trying to conceal her disgust for Katie's presence, and Katie continued to usurp her boss as necessary.

"I let them take her with a telepathic link in place," she stated plainly.

"So, she's with men who want to kill her for talking, and you think a telepathic link is gonna save her!?" Conwell shrieked.

"You needed a way to figure out where these guys are. Well, now we have a way for a witness to talk directly to us! To draw us a map!" Katie yelled back.

"Yeah, inside the head of a woman I don't trust!" Conwell countered.

"Then deal with your insecurities, and let's get these bastards!" Katie yelled.

"You have no authority on this team!" Conwell puffed out her chest.

"And one could argue that neither do you!" Katie stepped up.

"Sit down, and shut up," Conwell bit sternly. There was a flare behind her eye that no one had seen since the night she beat Barber to death with her bare hands, and it caused the team to shiver.

"No!" Katie roared before her hair turned silver once again.

Paper whirled around the office as her clothes faded away. Gray and brown swirls of air danced closely around Katie's body as she raised her hands out to her sides. She concentrated on the wind encompassing her fists, and she felt her entire emotional disposition wilt away as her windy hair danced wildly around her neck.

R.J. was petrified, Gio was rooted to the ground in shock, and Sean stared on in absolute captivation.

"Incredible," he breathed.

"You have your leads because of me this entire case!" Katie yelled as levitated off the ground. "You have had setback after setback, whereas I've provided nothing but answers to your blank spaces!"

Her wind-clouded body slowly inched closer to Conwell as the fire behind her eyes slowly died out.

"I am no more responsible for the death of your wife than you are responsible for the death of my family!"

And suddenly, as if in the blink of an eye, the papers all around the police station fluttered to the floor as Conwell stood, her eyes wide, and her jaw agape. Everyone in the room turned their eyes behind them, as wind-outlined wings stretched the span of the station flickered to life in flames of red and orange. Katie's hair, with windy wisps of gray and brown, soaked up red and orange streaks before her angry, hazel eyes turned to saddened yellow ones.

Her wind-draped figure sprung to life with fire as molten tears dripped down her cheeks. They carved deep indentations into her soft skin before her feet set back down onto the floor, and Conwell swallowed thickly before backing up from her form.

"I am so sorry for your loss," Katie choked out before she closed her eyes. She breathed deeply, trying desperately to get her emotional faculties under control before she mutated yet again, transforming back into the Katie they all knew.

However, Sean wished it wouldn't end.

He wanted to see all of her.

Every incarnation, and every color. Every transformation, and every emotion. He wanted to see the weight of her power as he soaked up her presence.

But, a voice ricocheted through Katie's head that pulled her back to the bowels of existence.

Angel, Claire breathed. *Angel, start writing. I know where we are.*

Katie grabbed quickly for a pen and paper as she began to jot down the words rolling through her head.

****

The team raced to the abandoned laboratory as Hernandez put several pieces in place. At first, he thought they were random, but he slowly pulled up name after name of people involved once the puzzle became clear to him, and it was easy to link them to the project now that he had been afforded a different starting point.

And all because of Katie's link with Claire.

We're coming, Claire, Katie breathed into her mind just as the SUV cut its lights off. *Just stay strong.* But, she started to become worried when Claire was no longer responding to her messages. "ETA?" she implored.

"3 minutes out," Conwell murmured. But, surprisingly, there was no edge to her voice.

The cars pulled up to the lab as everyone quietly jumped out, and Katie wrapped her hand around Sean's before they ducked away from the team, and went another route. She knew they could both take care of themselves if necessary, and the team splitting up could cover more ground.

"What's the plan?" Sean whispered.

The plan," Katie breathed into his mind before she smirked, *is to find Claire. She hasn't responded for the past 7 minutes.*

Sean's face filled with worry as they slowly approached a shrouded side door. He let go of his gun to reach out and turn the knob; but a flutter of green caught his eye. He gazed slowly over to Katie, and there she stood: with vibrant green eyes and flowing green and gold hair, and her clothes had now transformed once again into a flowing green gown that blossomed beautifully-scented flowers.

Earth? Sean breathed into her mind.

And all Katie did was nod.

They slowly made their way down the pitch-black hallway, and with every step they took she kept breathing into Claire's mind, desperate to get her to respond.

And yet, there was nothing.

Want some light? Katie breathed into Sean's mind. She felt his childlike anxiousness before her body switched gears. Soon, her flowing green and gold hair crackled with streaks of yellow and white fury; the living green dress turned into a pale yellow, and her eyes went white. She held up her hands as she levitated off the ground, and her electric wings spread wide down the hallway as she turned her body sideways. It illuminated the entire corridor as Sean's jaw physically unhinged, and he gazed over her body in wonder.

"Wow," he breathed.

"Let's find Claire," Katie whispered aloud as she tried to suppress the proud smile growing behind her cheeks.

She kept watch at her elevated post while Sean ducked into and cleared every room down the hallway. She slowly maneuvered with him to give him a decent amount of light, but the men's voices at the end of the hallway stopped them in their tracks and caused Katie to quickly revert back to her original form. She dropped to her feet silently as her emotions slowly ebbed back to rest.

"Boss give the word yet?" the man asked.

"Nah. Says he's got somethin' else for her before we kill 'er," the other man stated.

Katie swallowed hard before she closed her eyes and navigated towards Conwell's mind.

Laura, she breathed into her consciousness. *You can't talk back, but we have two men on the southside of the building talking about Claire. The person running the show has one last job for her before they kill her. Keep an eye out.*

She just finished giving the message when Sean grabbed her hand and ripped her down an opposing hallway.

"Message to someone?" Sean whispered lightly.

"Conwell," Katie whispered back.

"Oh. She's gonna love that." Sean smirked.

****

Conwell didn't fire the first shot until the entire lab was surrounded, and she knew Katie and Sean were safe from impact. People on the roof were aiming, people in the basement were coming up the steps, and people around all the sides of the building were penetrating the walls while flooding the hallways.

The problem with using regular human tactics, however, was that they never considered other solutions.

This was the main reason why Congress had passed the law that lead to Conwell being forced to hire Katie in the first place: too many regular men were dying in this line of work because of circumstances they simply couldn't foresee.

Katie ran through her mind all the abilities she knew Claire to have acquired over the years, because she had a sneaking suspicion they were going to try and use her to fight against them. Bullets flew from all directions as rooms were infiltrated. Sean and Katie split up to keep everyone safe while still looking for Claire, but no one had any idea where she was. Shot after shot rang out with bodies of scientists, and treasonous criminals dropping to the floor left and right. People were willing to die for a cause, rather than rat out a boss who would torture their lives; and so, blood spilled in endless amounts as Claire and Sean darted around the compound.

Katie knew her team would be geared towards finding that boss… but Katie was focused on finding Claire.

She switched back into Earth mode, and vines protruded from her wrists, and wrapped around the necks of unmarked mad men with machine guns. Her arms ripped them behind her body while she tossed them like dirty ragdolls, feeling the overwhelming sense of beauty that came with her earth form, and stomaching the sickness wafting through her system at the idea of utilizing her most beautiful form to kill.

What was raging in front of her, and what was raging inside of her, were so very different; and it was beginning to become too much for her to handle.

However, when Katie finally rounded the last corner to get to the center of the worn down laboratory- she had green hair billowing behind her, and flower petals gracing the train of her dress- her eyes peeled open in shock.

She found Claire... with a gun trained at the door entrance.

Pointing right at Katie.

Claire, Katie breathed into her mind as her earth gave way to fire. Her hair streaked out, and her eyes pale in their bright yellow state; all Claire did was smirk before she held the gun tighter in her hand.

"Angel," Claire mused lowly before she cocked her head.

What are you doing? Katie breathed before her fiery wings curled into her sides, and her dress slowly turned from green to red.

She eyeballed the serums that sat on shelves, painting the walls in their disgusting formulas, and she knew she would have to slowly heat up the room to destroy what was in there.

It would be easy to mask underneath her sadness.

"I'm honestly surprised you didn't seen it sooner, honestly," Claire said with a leer. "I mean, when they hauled me into the police station, besides internally laughing at their false sense of strength, I really, and truly thought I had been caught."

The lack of a double-pathway telepathic link between Katie and Conwell left her bereft of information Conwell had obtained from Hernandez before the infiltration began. Apparently, Hernandez had finally been able to pin down the constant bouncing of shell corporations to one steady constant. He'd managed to lock down a final bank account number that existed for longer than eight minutes.

Claire's background wasn't in teaching, like Katie had always been told… but was actually rooted in laboratory research. She didn't know any of this because the person standing in front of her was not actually Claire.

Katie watched, shocked and confused, as Claire continued to talk, and fire began to burn at her feet while molten tears sizzled down her cheeks. Claire's form slowly melted away and morphed into a random man she didn't recognize. She began to truly weep for the loss of her friend she had no idea was dead, and the temperature of the room slowly began to rise.

All Katie needed to do was get the room to 60 degrees and hold it.

"Had you probed my mind just a bit further," the man sneered, "it really would've been obvious."

"Even mutants must have boundaries," Katie argued.

"I wonder how your team will feel knowing that, if you had broken your own rules, we could've avoided so many deaths," the man hissed.

"What's the point?" Katie asked. "What's your endgame?

"Look," he commanded before he held his arms out wide to his sides.

Katie's eyes widened in horror as the strange man slowly morphed into Sean right before her very eyes.

"I'm living proof this serum works," Sean bellowed.

Or… at least… the man who had morphed into Sean.

She knew it wasn't Sean. She knew it wasn't her partner. She knew because she watched him transform.

And yet, she couldn't take her eyes off him.

"Oh, you like me, don't you?" fake-Sean said lowly before he lowered his gun to his side.

Katie swallowed hard at the prompting of that question.

"Would you like to know what it's like to... touch him?" fake-Sean smirked before his eyes darkened.

Katie's mouth dried as she watched the man slowly approach her. She had to stay rooted in the room because it had only just hit the temperature she needed to boil the serums in their glass cases, but this fake-Sean was towering over her, and his breath was hot on her face.

And it felt so good...

"To kiss him..." fake-Sean whispered before his hand came up to cup her molten cheek.

Katie couldn't help the involuntary nuzzle of her cheek into the palm of this man's hand as her mind became muddied with too many confused emotions.

"A horse to its water," fake-Sean whispered before he slowly lowered his lips to hers.

But, something inside of her snapped, like a rubber band to the skin. This was not Sean. She reared her hands back and planted them firmly onto his skin, searing her prints forever into his chest before she threw him backwards just as the serums along the walls began to bubble.

Mission accomplished.

"Screw you," Katie spat before her hands burst into flaming balls of fire that roared within the palms of her hands.

"As you wish," the man smirked before he quickly morphed back into his old form. He brought the gun back up to Katie's level, aimed it as her chest, and pulled the trigger.

Katies eyes widened with the harsh crack of the bullet leaving the barrel, and the fire in her palms died out.

****

The crack of the gun silenced Katie's roaring emotions for a split second. The fire died from the palms of her hands, and her vision blurred with hot, molten tears as she watched a body shoot in front of her.

"No!" she shrieked.

She watched as Sean peeled himself from the floor, and his blood dripped down the wounds of his chest. Cursing, he stared down his body, and one by one, the bullets popped free of the wounds, making sickening wet sounds as every last one came free. Just as the last one dinged to the floor, the glass vials all around the room began to burst.

"No," the man, whispered in disbelief. "No! No! What have you done!" The mystery man looked around him in horror as he took in the busted glass, and tainted serum soaking the floor all around him. He was too distracted to notice the other agents charge in, and open fire when he wouldn't drop the gun.

Bullets ripped through his shoulders and caused the gun to fall from his hand while he howled in pain.

"Katie," Sean whipped around before he looked her up and down. "You alright?"

But all Katie could do was drop her eyes to the massive blood stain soaking Sean's shirt. He'd taken those bullets for her. Just like that.

"My serum works! I've made our evolutionary advancement available to everyone!" The madman roared as Conwell ran to handcuff him. "I am a genius. The world needs to know of my greatness!" he shrieked as Conwell yelled at him to shut up and read him his rights.

"Not really," Katie finally managed to say as she reached out for the man and pulled him into her arms.

The mystery man took one last look at the rest of his vials breaking, bubbling on the floor as its substance seeped into the cracks, and his shriek of horror echoed through the hallways of the abandoned warehouse; Gio came up to help restrain him.

"No! My vials! My serum! Do you have any idea what you've done!?" the man shrieked.

"Yeah," Katie murmured before she turned slowly back to Sean. "I do."

She slowly settled back into her original form as steam rose from her skin. It poured from between her lips, and out through her nostrils. As the carved tear trails slowly began to heal themselves from her thick, hot tears, Sean put his hand on her back to help calm her.

"Good job, Smaug," he said with a smirk.

"I think I like Angel better," Katie fired back.

"I didn't honestly think this case would be so quick," R.J. mused as Katie and Sean watched agents walk innocent mutants out from another set of double doors, where she caught a glimpse of cages they'd been held in. Some of them seemed too stunned to realize they were free of this madhouse to show much emotion.

"They're usually not this quick?" Katie asked.

"Never." Sean chuckled.

Katie looked up into his eyes and found that same intense calm that flooded her when the mystery man had morphed into him. It was like the lazy sloshing of waves on a cool fall morning at the edge of a beach.

"Sean...I—"

She cut herself off, feeling a strong pull to tell him what had happened. About the transformation. About the touch. About how she felt.

About how much she had wanted to kiss him.

Sean watched her intently, locking his eyes with hers before he turned his body completely towards her. She dipped her gaze to the floor, unable to come up with the adequate words for the situation.

And it was then that another question came barreling into her mind.

"Where the hell is Claire?" Katie whispered.

R.J. and Sean traded looks before Katie lifted her gaze and began heading for the exit.

"I have to find Claire," she said.

"Then let me come with you." Sean reached out for Katie's arm. "R.J. can help Gio and Conwell with all of this back here."

"Ah, our little children have grown up," Katie quipped.

The chuckle that poured from between Sean's lips made her neck warm, and she almost pulled him in for a kiss right then and there.

"Where do we start?" Sean asked.

"Her cabin," Katie said before she turned her body, and started for the exit once again. "We start at her cabin."

****

Katie had no idea what she would find at Claire's cabin, but she knew it wasn't her body. Claire's corpse was probably locked up in a lab somewhere, waiting to be found by someone on her team. But she knew she couldn't be there to see it, and Sean understood that.

"You know it's not your fault, right?" He asked while Katie ran her hand along the back of her couch. "You couldn't have possibly known."

"I would've if I had just broken my self-imposed boundaries," Katie spat.

"But those boundaries make you who you are," he stressed. "We all have them."

He watched as Katie mindlessly walked across the room. She was breathing in the scent of the home, knowing it was a place she would probably never return, and his heart ached for her.

"She had no family, you know," Katie said softly. "She was adopted, then cast out when they found her mutant abilities emerging."

Sean felt his blood boil at that admission.

"She worked, and struggled for everything she had, and she was damn proud of it."

"You knew her much better than you let us on, didn't you?" Sean asked. He walked up to her from behind slowly, not wanting to startle her fragile state, and he reached his hand out and put it comfortingly on her shoulder.

"I guess," Katie whispered. All she was trying to do was keep her tears at bay, even though they eventually went cascading down her cheeks.

Sean watched her tears in awe as they turned a molten red; and he addressed her again. "How did you know her?" He felt Katie's body heat radiating dozens of degrees above where it should have been, and he ripped his hand back as her hair slowly draped itself in a fiery orange.

"She was my childhood best friend," Katie choked out.

At that admission, Sean threw his arms around Katie. He turned her around and grit his teeth at her pain while he slunk his arms around her body and held her close. Katie's molten tears flowing down her face burned trails into the fabric of Sean's clothing, and as her hands came up to cup the tattered fabric of his shirt, her light whimpers grew into heaving sobs.

Katie lost her best friend.

Her heart was breaking in half.

****

The cases continued to pour in, and the team continued to solve them at mind-blowing speeds. Conwell's walls finally began to melt towards Katie as the two of them interacted, and Conwell came to trust the untrustworthy mutant on her team after a mere three months of working on the job. Soon, Katie was being invited over for team dinners, and girl's nights; Conwell had even invited her over a couple of times so the two of them could talk. Her boss had many questions about her abilities, and Katie was open to educating her on them.

As always, the holidays came and went, and Valentine's Day approached. Everyone on Katie's team started talking about their plans, while she stayed silent on the matter.

"I'm headed over to Gio's, actually," she heard Conwell say. "He's cookin' and then we're gonna look at some case files."

"Really? Work on Valentine's Day?" Katie crinkled her nose.

"Trust me, it's not uncommon," R.J. smirked.

"Well, I've got me a hot date. I'm cookin' dinner, I'm lightin' candles, I'm buyin' wine…" Hernandez trailed off.

"Just make sure to wrap it up!" Gio called out.

"Gross." Katie smirked.

"What are your plans, Katie?" Sean asked.

"Gotta date with Mack," she mused.

"Oh, who's Mack?" Hernandez exclaimed before he bounded over and cocked his hip up onto her desk.

"Mack? Someone's got a Mack!? Is Mack handsome? Is he muscular? Is he luscious?" R.J. rambled on.

Katie would have laughed had it not been for the reaction on Sean's face that caught her eye. She saw his face fall at the mention of Mack, and her stomach churned with something akin to guilt.

"Don't get too excited, Hernandez," she said lovingly, "Mack is my friendly little play toy."

Hernandez roared with laughter at her desk while R.J.'s face blushed with embarrassment.

"Really? You just asked if the man I was dating was 'luscious', and now you're blushing because I mentioned a toy?" Katie giggled.

"So, you don't have a boyfriend?" Sean asked lightly.

"Not unless you're askin', hot stuff," Katie purred with a wink.

The sentiment tumbled from Katie's lips with ease, and everyone in the room slowly turned towards Sean to watch his reaction.

"What was that!?" Gio called from across the room.

"I told 'em he was hot!" Katie yelled back.

And all the while, Sean's complexion reddened with embarrassment. His eyes widened with wonder, and happiness; he couldn't help the grin that spread across his face, and he finally found the courage to ask her what they both were waiting for since Claire's case.

"Well, if you don't have plans," he began, "maybe you'd like to come over Saturday."

"Oh, Scott's got game!" Hernandez smiled.

"I'll cook the food?" He asked as his eyes implored Katie impatiently.

"Then… I guess I'll bring the wine," Katie mused lightly.

"And Mack! Take Mack, too!" Hernandez shouted before he clamored off her desk. Katie's face dropped, and R.J. laughed hysterically; Conwell couldn't help but shake her head as she watched her mutant colleague reach for a pen to chuck it at their technical analyst.

Katie missed Hernandez's head by an inch, but he still exaggeratedly barreled through the massive double doors.

****

Katie smoothed out her dress and tousled her hair one last time. She was nervous, though she knew there was no reason to be. With the bag of wine clenched tightly within her fist, and the decadent dessert she had made cradled in the other, she drew in one more deep breath before she raised the hand with the wine to knock lightly on Sean's apartment door.

She heard a bit of shuffling, a thud, some silent cursing, and then the doorknob turned. A tall and disheveled Sean stood on the other side, smiling broadly at her, and Katie couldn't help but rake her eyes down his body before they stopped at his chest.

There was an inscription on the apron he was wearing, and she chuckled at it, and crooked an eyebrow. She stood lightly onto her tiptoes, put her hand lightly onto Sean's shoulder, and kissed his cheek. Sean blushed furiously underneath the warmth of her lips, and she settled herself back down onto her feet.

"If you insist," Katie shrugged.

"Insist what?" Sean asked.

Katie only pointed to his apron and it caused Sean to let out a breathy chuckle, embarrassingly ripping it over his head.

"Whoops," he said lowly.

"Gag gift?" Katie asked as she entered Sean's apartment and set the bag down onto his kitchen counter.

"Gio got it for me for my birthday last year," Sean smiled. "He uh… thought it would be funny since I couldn't cook at the time."

"Knowing Gio, he probably thought it would get you laid." She even threw in a playful wink just to watch Sean squirm. "Well, whatever you're cooking," she said before she took in a deep breath through her nose, "smells absolutely wonderful."

"Thanks! It's actually a recipe Conwell recommended."

"Seriously?" Katie asked. "Did you ask Gio for the wine pairings?"

"You caught me red-handed." Sean playfully held his hands in the air.

Katie giggled before she reached for the corkscrew she brought and began to work the cork out of the top of the bottle while Sean went to go hunt down a couple of wine glasses.

"I took the liberty of stopping in at the bakery down the road to get this," she said as she nodded to the dessert.

As Sean filled both the wine glasses with the beautiful crimson liquid, Katie pulled out a box from the bag that soon filled the room with the scent of cinnamon and chocolate. She opened the lid to reveal two perfectly-decorated tiramisu personal cakes, and they were both in the shape of a heart.

"You walked here?" Sean asked.

"It's not that far. Plus, I like the fresh air."

"It's supposed to rain later tonight..." Sean trailed off worriedly.

"You mean you aren't ripping my clothes off on Valentine's Day weekend and bedding me until I beg for mercy?" Katie asked, eyeing him closely.

Sean almost dropped his glass down onto the floor as he choked on his sip of wine.

"I'm just playin'," Katie winked.

She grabbed her wine glass and held it up to Sean in a mock-toast before taking a long pull from the glass, and the entire time Sean watched her lips wrap around the edge of the glass.

"I have an entire side of me that's water, Sean. A little rain never hurt. If it rains while I'm walking home, I'll survive."

The nervous chuckle that peeled from between Sean's lips caused a smirk to appear on Katie's cheeks.

"Thank you for inviting me over for dinner," she mused.

"Thank you for coming," Sean finally said when he found his voice.

"You'll have to forgive me," Katie breathed before she held out her arms, "but I've never done this before."

"You've never been on a date?" Sean asked.

"Is this a date?" Katie countered.

"I mean, if you want it to be, it is," Sean nervously stated.

"Well, I'm under the impression that it is," Katie winked.

She loved watching him squirm underneath her gaze. She brought the wine glass back to her lips and polished off her glass, and he couldn't take his eyes off her as she lightly moaned with the decadent taste of the wine caressing her tongue.

"Good," Sean whispered.

"What I meant was, I've never done Valentine's Day before," Katie finally clarified.

"Well, neither have I, unless you count celebrating it with your mom. I did that a lot when I was a kid."

"Do you love your mom?" Katie asked.

"More than words," Sean sighed. She watched him smile as an alarm went off in the kitchen, and her eyes trailed after him as he opened the oven door. One by one, he pulled out a roast and vegetables that he sat in the middle of the table in his living area, and the smells of dinner caused her mouth to water before she grabbed the opened bottle of wine and sat it down amidst all the delectable foods.

"Well, if you love your mom," Katie began again, "then it counts. Valentine's Day isn't just romantic... it's also full of love. That part's important, I think."

She took the liberty of refilling her glass before Sean stuck his empty one in her purview.

"She would like you," Sean mused.

"Hmm?" Katie hummed.

"My mom. She'd like you," Sean said again.

"Is your mother a mutant?"

"No. But she does find them fascinating," he offered. She couldn't help but clock the slight twinge of sadness that slipped through his eyes, and for a split second she wanted to ask about his father. But she decided against it and continued with the conversation as is.

"Is there anything else we need before we sit down?" Katie asked.

"No, I just need to find some matches…" he trailed off as he began to pat down his body.

"Oh, Sean," Katie chuckled, "looks like that memory of yours needs a refresher course."

She held her fingers over the unlit candlesticks that adorned the table for two, and when she snapped her fingers, a little flame danced between them. Sean looked on in awe as the candles lit, and the light they cast played seductively off the curves of Katie's body before she brought her fingers to her lips and blew them out.

"There." She smiled before her eyes found their way back to Sean's.

And she committed the look to memory, silently hoping that, one day soon, she would be able to elicit it from him again.

****

Valentine's Day went very well for the both. Dinner was incredible, the wine was potent, and the conversation flowed between Katie and Sean with slim-to-no lulls. The two of them chatted about childhood memories, and Katie regaled him with stories of her parents before everything spiraled out of control. Sean opened a bit about his relationship with his mother and how tumultuous it was with her having Alzheimer's. He even told Katie about his father, and how he left them when he was very young; and that he never did get over how angry he was with him for abandoning them.

When the evening began to wind down, Katie found herself a bit disappointed when she had to leave.

The girls teased her about it, making mention of wanting the "dirty details," and wanted to know if Sean "talked nasty in bed." Katie just shoved away their comments while shaking her head and giggling. She kept telling them it was just dinner and good conversation, but they were having none of it.

Sean was getting it just as bad from the guys.

"It's never just dinner and wine," Gio warned lowly.

"You didn't even ask her to stay?" Conwell asked.

"Geez, boss!" Sean had yelped, causing a ruckus of laughter to drift from Conwell's office. "No, I didn't. It wasn't raining, and we weren't too drunk from the wine, so when we were done, we talked while we cleaned up and then she went home."

"You gonna ask her out again?" Gio prodded.

"Well… we sorta came back to a case, so I haven't really—"

"Did you tell her you had a nice time?" Conwell interjected.

"I mean… I couldn't find my phone that night so—"

"Jesus, Scott, did you even kiss her goodbye on the cheek!?" Gio asked breathlessly.

"What is with you guys?" Sean yelped. He stormed out of Conwell's office as everyone else turned to look up at him, and Katie's worried eyes followed him all the way out of the office before she slowly turned back to everyone up on the balcony.

They had stirred up a self-conscious part of Sean's mind, and he wasn't sure how he would fix things.

Were things even broken?

He wasn't sure anymore.

Did Katie not have a good time? Was he rude to not invite her to stay? Did she want to stay the night!?

But, over in Katie's mind, she was turning over the events of the entire evening while she relished in the look he had given her over dinner. Katie enjoyed the conversation, specifically the fact that none of the conversation had come back around to her mutant powers. Maybe that was because Sean was a mutant himself, but it was refreshing to be around someone who wanted to know other things about her besides the "things she could do". Not only that, but Sean hadn't "fetishized" her because of her mutant abilities, and she found it odd in a good way that he hadn't wanted her to sleep over after the first date.

Not that she wouldn't have turned him down… but it was nice. It was the first time Katie had ever experienced someone who wanted to be around just her.

Not her powers.

Katie decided she wanted to express that somehow. She wanted to get him to understand that the dinner was so much more than just a friendly date to her. In her eyes, that Valentine's dinner had become the date that she would now hold all dates up to in comparison, and that was a massive deal to her.

She hadn't had one of those before.

But, when she finally got the courage to pull Sean aside to tell him, she saw that same strange look in his eyes, and it worried her.

"Sean?" she asked lightly. "Are you alright?"

He stayed silent before his eyes lightly began darting around, and Katie took the lead and pulled him into a corner, away from everyone's prying eyes.

"Talk to me," she asked gently. "What's going on?"

Sean brought his eyes level to hers, and the panic that she once saw slowly subsided into a twinge of sadness.

"Don't make me pull it out of you..." Katie threatened lowly.

"Were you expecting to have sex Valentine's weekend?" Sean blurted out.

He must have said it loud, because both Gio and Conwell groaned around the corner. But, the face Katie made at the question was priceless, and it caused Sean to laugh in relief. Pretty soon, that laughter sparked Katie's giggling, and the tension that was brewing between them melted away as the two of them began laughing together.

Just like it had always been.

"Don't let them get in your head," Katie giggled. "Sometimes people do things like what you did Valentine's weekend to get sex. But, you do things like that because you want to. I like that about you."

"That's not true!" Gio protested before he stepped around the corner. "I treat my ladies well."

"And I treat them with respect," Conwell protested before she, too, stepped out from around the corner.

"Sean," Katie started again. "I wasn't expecting sex, and I wasn't disappointed with the evening. I enjoyed every second I spent with you. I felt...like you actually wanted to be with me, not just my abilities."

"Of course, I want to be with you," Sean said as he held Katie's hands within his. "It's why I asked you to dinner."

Katie's heart fluttered within the confines of her chest as a thankful smile ricocheted across her cheeks.

"And," Sean said, shifting on his feet, "if, um…you're not too busy this Saturday, maybe we could have dinner again?"

Katie sensed the entire team gathered behind her back, listening and waiting for her answer; a twinge of red flushed heartily down her neck and heated her back.

"I'll cook," Katie mused lowly.

"And I'll bring the wine."

****

Katie was in the middle of cooking shrimp and steak on her countertop griddle when she heard a tentative knock sound through her place. She placed her spatula down and outstretched her arm, and a vine slowly protruded from her wrist and headed towards the knob of the door.

"Come on in!" she shouted as the vines twirled around the knob and opened the door.

Katie giggled at the shock that rolled over Sean's face. Even though he was a mutant, he never ceased to be shocked with what she could do, and it sent a light flurry of excitement through her body before she went back to cooking.

"Hey there." Sean smiled as he placed his bag on the countertop. "Got some nice wine recommendations from Gio."

"Beautiful." She tossed the rice and vegetables in the soy sauce and honey mixture she had created, and Sean couldn't help but salivate as the smells flowed through her home.

"You have a mini hibachi restaurant in your kitchen," Sean smirked.

"And I'm almost done." Katie winked back. She scooped up the food and divvied it up between two massive dinner plates, and Sean decided to start opening drawers and cabinets to set the table for the dinner.

"Red or white?" Sean asked.

"Oh, you didn't have to set the table. I was gonna do that!" Katie exclaimed while she turned around with both plates in her hands.

"Red... or white?" Sean asked again with a very serious look on his face he only managed to hold for a moment before they both laughed.

"Red, please."

Katie walked and placed the plates on the table and her ears rang out as the sound of the wine hitting the glass filled the corners of her kitchen. Sean had apparently found everything, because napkins as well as forks donned the table, and when she sat the plates of food down onto the wooden surface, he handed her a glass of wine.

"Thank you for having me over for dinner," Sean said sincerely before taking a sip from his glass.

"Thank you for bringing me alcohol," Katie said with a smirk.

The two of them stared at each other for a while and Katie felt the beginnings of a tingle start in her toes. The light in the kitchen overhead flickered, and she closed her eyes before she took a deep breath.

"Everything okay?" Sean asked as he cocked an eyebrow up on his face.

"Just fine," Katie breathed.

But she knew herself better than that.

She knew this dinner would be rough.

As the two of them ate, the conversation easily flowed again. Katie talked about what she enjoyed about the city, and Sean talked about his favorite places to go when he wasn't at work. He asked if she had celebrated the holidays, and then he regaled her with his trip to Las Vegas to be with his mom over Thanksgiving. Katie couldn't stop smiling at him, and the two of them hardly touched their food during the first hour of the conversation.

And then she felt it.

A very slight sensation running up against her leg that sent a welcome shiver down her spine. The lights flickered above them yet again before Sean pulled his foot back.

"How is your mother doing?" Katie asked, trying to change the subject.

Sean's face dropped slightly before he cleared his throat. "She's fine. Getting the best care she can get," he quipped.

"You know, if you ever wanna talk ab—"

"I said she's fine," Sean murmured.

"Well, if you don't wanna talk about it, but it starts bothering you, you can always come here and sit in silence," Katie offered. She couldn't imagine how it felt for Sean to watch his mother lose all their memories. Alzheimer's ravaged the mind in a way that was painful, even for the person experiencing it, and she knew Sean would one day look at his mother and she wouldn't recognize him.

The thought broke her soul.

Sean stared at her for an unnerving amount of time after her offer. She sipped her glass of wine cautiously, not wanting to irritate him any more than she had, and just as she was going to excuse herself to the bathroom, Sean finally spoke up.

"Thank you," he said genuinely. "Really."

"If you come over, I won't make you talk. Just know you have a space here if you can't stand being at home," Katie said before she picked up her fork.

"That means a great deal to me," Sean said quietly. He reached out to grasp her hand, making his thumb dance in light circles on her skin. Her eyes flashed yellow for a split second before she grabbed ahold of her own emotions.

But not before Sean caught it.

"Katie?" he asked.

His voice- low and inquiring- caused Katie to close her eyes as white sparks began to fly off the end of the fork she was holding.

But all Sean did was grip her hand tighter. "Are you alright?" he asked.

She heard it in his voice: part of him was fearful and part of him was curious. When she opened her eyes and slowly looked over towards him, her hair flickered to shades of yellow and white before sparks ignited between the tendrils of her hair.

For most people, it's simply referred to as a "spark", a moment where- for a fraction of a second- they feel the strongest pulse of electricity blow through their body at someone's touch, or voice, or presence. But, for someone like Katie who could actually wield electricity, a "spark" through her conductive body was like setting a flicker of flame onto a gasoline-soaked log in a fireplace.

Sean watched in awe as he slowly pulled his hand back. His eyes raked over her energized hair and jumped at the sparks flying from her fork. Katie's body visibly turned into a shining conductive electrical masterpiece; yet another element he hadn't seen slowly came into form upon her body.

Her clothes molded into a flowing yellow dress that hugged her body and crackled with every movement. He stood when she pushed her chair back to stand herself. He was hooked on her eyes: the beautiful pale yellow taking his breath away as Katie continued to stare at him, and as he continued to take in her form, his eyes simply grew wider with awe.

"Excuse me," Katie choked out.

Her energy was getting the best of her and she knew she had to get herself under control. She rushed off to the bathroom and took the tension with her, as she left, all of the lights in her home went off. Sean stood, gaping in her direction, in the darkened home.

Katie shut herself in the bathroom and leaned over the sink, taking deep breaths while she closed her eyes. She had to get this surge of uncontrolled energy back under control or risk ruining the rest of the night, and she desperately wanted Sean to stay.

Anything to get him to stay.

Slowly but surely, her body calmed down and her form changed back: her sparkling yellow dress morphed back into the little black sundress she had chosen for the evening, and her eyes settled back to their original color as her hair stopped sparking.

That was going to be a problem with Sean if she couldn't learn to control it.

It startled her, how quickly she had lost control. Usually she closed her eyes and conjured the element, and emotions just rose from the conjuring. There was only one other time her emotions had ricocheted so out of control that her transformation was prompted rather than asked for. And that only other time had been when Katie's fiery wings spread uncontrollably and burned down the scientific facility she had been held at as a child. Her sadness had completely overcome her existence after her parents had been killed, and her grief was so encompassing that her wings spread without her knowledge.

Yet again, she was losing control to a man that her body, and mind, found irresistible.

"Katie?" Sean asked before a light knock came at the door. "Are you okay?"

The same surge of energy deep within the pit of her stomach swelled at just the sound of his voice, but this time she was able to concentrate on it and keep it at bay, buried deep within her, before she opened her mouth to answer.

"Yes. I'm uh…I'm alright. Just…let me splash some water in my face."

Even she realized just how idiotic that sounded.

"You could always just transform into water and slap yourself with your wing," Sean mused lightly. The mental image his statement created caused Katie to giggle, and when she reached for the doorknob she was standing face-to-face with a broad-smiling, wholly-towering, calm and collected Sean Scott.

"I'm sorry," Katie offered after her giggling stopped. "It's been a…"

The sigh that peeled from Katie's lips prompted Sean to hold out her glass of wine to her.

"Refilled it just for you," he said with a gently smile. "It's been what?" He prompted lightly after Katie took her glass from his hand.

"It's been a long time," she struck up again, "since my energies have spurred my elements."

"I've realized it doesn't happen often," Sean commented.

"It doesn't happen ever," Katie corrected.

"What energy happened?"

The question caused Katie to choke on her wine before she began to cough lightly. "Come again?" she choked out.

"I said," Sean chuckled before he brought the back of his hand to wipe some stray wine off Katie's cheek, "what energy prompted the reaction? What's associated with 'electricity'?"

Katie's heart pounded deep within her chest so hard she thought her ribs would crack. Her breathing became sharper underneath the darkness of her home, and she closed her eyes before she drew in a shaking breath.

It was now or never, and she didn't ever want to find herself lying to Sean.

He was too perfect for that.

"Sexual energy," Katie admitted. "The energy that veered out of control was sexual."

She started at Sean's chest before she slowly felt him remove the wine glass from her hand. Her eyes slowly panned up to his unblinking eyes, and he couldn't help but take in the electric blue that was still visibly flickering behind Katie's naturally-brown eyes. The lights in her home continued to flicker as Katie's body drained them for her own selfish purposes, and as the two of them held each other's gaze, he quickly drained both wine glasses down his throat before dropping them to the floor and wrapping his arms around Katie's waist.

He closed the gap between the two of him as Katie threw her arms around his neck, and suddenly their feet were off the floor. Katie's electric wings carried them back to her bedroom as their dinner grew cold and inedible; the energy that surged throughout Katie's body physically shook her in Sean's arms as their bodies slowly descended onto the top of her bed.

In her dark, silent home, Katie's wings wrapped wholly around Sean's body, and pressed him deeper into her touch. Her hair crackled on top of the comforter of the bed as Sean's lips slowly trailed down her neck; time was racing for her. It felt as if the clock was spinning itself on the wall as their electrified bodies tangled in the sheets and rolled to the floor; with every pulse of electricity that ricocheted through Katie's body, Sean moaned and groaned as he explored every single inch of her. Their love for one another kept the rhythmic pace that encouraged them on all through the evening, and the electricity that should have lit up Katie's house surged within every atom of her body as she held Sean close. They spent the evening getting to know one another in the most intimate of ways, and when the two of them were tired and spent. They fell asleep safe in each other's arms. But little did Katie know that the morning would bring a horrific sight. One she would pay for in the weeks to come.

She fluttered her eyes open and took in the bright morning light streaming through her window. She stretched her body out before she felt Sean's hand fall from her side and onto the bed. His lazy movement caused her to turn over and press her naked body into his, and she smiled through her sleepy gaze when she realized he had stayed. He had actually stayed the night with her.

"Morning," Sean croaked.

"Morning." Katie smiled.

"How're you feeling?" Sean asked.

Katie furrowed her brow at how he sounded. His speech was a bit off and his words seemed a bit slurred. When she sat up and took a look at Sean's face, horror ricocheted through every molecule of her mutant being. His smile was crooked, and his eye was lazy.

"Sore..." Katie trailed off. "Sean, are you alright?"

"Of... course..." Sean said.

At least, that's what Katie thought he said.

Katie watched as Sean tried to roll over towards her, and when his face fell uncontrollably as he tried to look at her, panic exploded within her. She scrambled out of bed and threw on the first pair of clothes she found on her floor before she rushed around to Sean's side and threw his good arm around her shoulders.

"We gotta get clothes on you," Katie breathed while Sean attempted to say something to her.

But his speech had devolved into nonsensical syllables as his body began to deteriorate in front of her eyes.

She knew what was happening. She knew exactly what had gone wrong and she chastised herself as she slipped on his clothes. She had thrown away everything she knew to be true about herself for one selfish moment of passion, and now the one man who had been selfless enough to let her in was going to die.

Sean was going to die because of her. Her electricity from the night before had short-circuited his body's own electrical currents... and he was having a stroke.

****

Katie stumbled through the emergency hospital doors and saw R.J. already there. She scrambled to help Katie get Sean onto a gurney while tears continued to pour down Sean's face, and Katie physically felt her heart break before R.J. looked up and asked the question.

"What the hell happened?"

"That's a good question," Conwell said as she approached quickly with Gio in tow. But Sean was already being wheeled away and everyone recognized the shirt Katie was wearing.

She was wearing Sean's shirt.

And the tears that poured forth from Katie's eyes stained Sean's work shirt before they slowly turned into molten lava drops that burned through her heated skin.

****

The team sat in the waiting room with their legs jiggling and their pacing nerves as Katie sat off in a corner. She was staring blankly at the wall, wishing to the heavens above a doctor would come through those double doors and tell her Sean was alive.

A hand lay down between her shoulder blades, and the sensation caused her to jump; she whipped her head over and saw Gio smiling sympathetically. He took in the burned tear trails as her eyes were still crying, and it wasn't until he pulled his hand away quickly from her burning skin that he finally opened his mouth.

"You couldn't have known," he soothed.

"It's basic anatomy, Gio," Katie snapped, furious with herself. "If you jolt a heart while it's down, it starts. If you jolt it while it's up, it shuts down."

"It didn't shut Sean down," he urged.

"No, it just fried half his brain and inhibited an entire side of his body from moving," she spat.

"Agent Sean Scott?"

Katie leapt to her feet at the doctor's call before she rushed over to where he was standing. His gaze met hers and she sighed with relief. The doctor was a mutant, and surely, he was more than capable of aiding another mutant.

"Agent Scott has suffered a massive electrical surge to over 60% of his body," the doctor informed them.

Everyone gazed at Katie before her eyes turned orange. She had never felt this out of control in her life, and she was scared that if her sadness raged any further, she would only put more lives at risk.

Like with the scientific experimentation building when she was little.

"What... how...is he?"

"His brain is fine," the doctor urged. "He's all there and nothing has been damaged on that front."

"On that front?" Conwell questioned.

"Despite his powers, his body's still struggling. The right side of his face is lagging, almost like he had a stroke, and his left arm and left leg are almost unresponsive."

The muffled sobs Katie tried to hold back were pouring through her muted lips, and she sank to her knees before R.J. bent down next to her and tried to comfort her. No one could touch her, what with her skin on fire, and everyone watched as her hair turned red. They had to physically back up to not be burned by the heat radiating from her body.

"He's going to need regular physical therapy to begin getting his mobility back until his powers kick in. Part of the brain that was damaged is the part of the brain that controls the chemical reactions that make a mutant a mutant. In a few months, he should be able to fully return to work."

"A few months?" Gio breathed.

Katie's muffled sobs grew to body-wracking heaves, and her own sorrow drowned out the rest of what everyone else was saying as her sadness boiled over the top. She knew she had to pull herself together, to get herself back on even footing if she ever had any chance of going back and seeing Sean. She was struggling to simply breathe, and it felt as if her heart was physically being ripped from her chest.

"When…can I…see…him?" She hiccupped.

"I take it you're Katie?" the doctor asked.

She wiped her nose and shaking, rose to her feet. When she raised her orange eyes up to the doctor, he assessed the bloodied trails on her face that were becoming ingrained from the molten lava tears she was crying.

"Yes," Katie whispered.

And she watched sorrow fill the doctor's eyes as her worst nightmare was imagined right there in the middle of the hot hospital waiting room.

"He has requested not to see you at this time."

****

Sean spent three weeks in the hospital, and Katie felt as if she was living a nightmare. He refused to see her and she couldn't stand to be in her home without thinking of him. She wanted so badly to take his hand…to hold him and tell him how sorry she was for not foreseeing the consequences of losing herself in him that night. She wanted to whisper in his ear and tell him she was going to be there every step of the way, and that he wasn't going to lose her.

Never lose her.

But, she settled for sending him handwritten letters that were addressed to his room. She settled for having regularly-timed flowers sent to his bedside that provided beautiful smells for his astringent-filled hospital room while she sat in her home and burned deeper trails of pain down her face. She called the hospital many times to check up on him, but she was only fed sparse details from R.J. Sean had left her as his main medical liaison, and the only reason she was getting the information she was getting was because R.J. felt sympathy for her.

"He smiled for the first time yesterday."

"He's already gaining a bit of movement back in his fingertips."

"He squeezed my hand!"

She wanted to be there for all those moments. All those firsts that were so monumental to Sean's development. But, she settled for hearing about them from the team.

Finally, the day came for him to be released. Everyone was there, and Katie wanted to be there so desperately. To surprise him by his car and tell him she was taking him home and not leaving until he was walking on both of his feet again.

She missed her work partner desperately.

But, the team advised her that it would probably be too much for him, and all Katie could do was put in for time off work. She couldn't stand to walk by his desk and he not be there. She couldn't stand to look up at the empty offices and know where everyone was.

The one place she wasn't allowed to go.

"Just let him come around in his own time," Gio soothed.

"He'll be lonely in his apartment and call for you, I'm sure," R.J. consoled.

"It's like a victim seeing the person who hurt them. Just give him some time," Conwell said a bit too bluntly and earned an annoyed look from Gio.

Great.

Just great.

Three days had gone by since Sean had gone home, and not a single word had been summoned her way. He dodged Katie's phone calls and never once asked her to come over, and soon all communication on her part ceased. She felt lost. Lost in a sea of endless emotion she hadn't felt since she had lost her parents. She didn't allow herself the option of loving anyone until Sean came along, and while she wasn't ready to utter that word just yet, she also knew he was the first person she had actively cared for strongly enough for their detriment to ruin her.

Sink her.

Swallow her whole.

And as she sank back into the chair she had dragged into her room, her eyes fluttered closed, and she watched the sunlight dip below the tree line just outside of her home.

She didn't care if she ever returned to work.

****

Conwell understood when Katie asked for time off. No one on the team could imagine the grief she was experiencing, and even though she threw herself into the cases they had gotten since Sean's admittance into the hospital, they knew it was because she didn't want to think about home.

About the reality of the downside to her powers.

Katie sulked around in bed and never felt like eating. She stopped calling Sean's phone just to hear his voicemail talk to her, and she stopped leaving the begging and pleading messages that clamored for his presence again. She walked around in a constant daze. Her greasy red hair was piled high on her head, and her molten lava tears had started to leave scarring trails down her cheeks. They carved their way into her skin and left permanent indentations, and when she dared to go into public she kept a hoodie pulled tightly over her head while she aimed her head down and walked aimlessly around the city.

She had stayed hot in her fire of sadness for so long that steam was beginning to permanently rise from her skin.

But fate was about to step in and give her a second chance.

Give them both a second chance.

Katie sighed heavily before she stopped in front of a random building. She sniffled in the sadness as another barrage of molten tears slipped their way through the carved valleys on her cheeks, and as she craned her neck back to take in the beauty of the old building, a black puff of smoke emersed from between her lips.

The shocked gasp of a recognizable voice behind her caused her to whip her aching body around.

"Sean," she breathed.

Her puffy, cracked orange eyes slowly took in the familiar set of eyes, and she found Sean leaning on a cane, upright on his own two feet as he carried a takeout bag of food in his free hand. She saw the lack of sleep Sean had been getting. There were dark rings under his eyes, his hair was long and unkempt, and his body was trembling just to keep himself upright on the cane.

To support a leg that still hadn't been healed by his own mutant powers.

Katie finally looked back to his eyes, and what she saw was not what she expected to see: instead of seeing disgust and anger, she saw relief and guilt. She furrowed her brow while she studied his stare, and as she was looking, Sean took a tentative step forward. He put his food on the ground, reached his arm out towards her, and encompassed her shoulders just before he laid his chin down onto the top of her head.

He was hugging her.

After an entire month of not seeing him, Sean was hugging Katie.

"Oh, god Sean," Katie choked out. She wrapped her arms around him and held him close, and a sense of calm washed over her before the reality of her emotions came flooding back to her.

"Why didn't you want to see me?" she croaked.

Sean released her and pushed her out, and for a split-second Katie thought he was intentionally pushing her away. She cursed herself for even asking the question, but before she could reach out for him and beg him to stay, his low voice hit her eardrums with an answer that left her rooted in shock.

"I knew you would feel guilty," he said.

My god, she had missed his voice.

"Of course, I would have," Katie said. "I still do."

"You couldn't have known…" Sean trailed off.

"Yes, I should've of. There's no excuse.".

She was so confused. The reaction she thought Sean should have with her was not the one being administered, and her entire mind whirled with confusion.

"I'm not mad at you," Sean whispered.

"Why not?" Katie whispered back. She shook her head firmly as she stared at his chest, until his finger crooked up underneath her chin and pulled her gaze up to his.

"Because you couldn't have known," he stated again.

"You should be furious," Katie said. "You should be angry, and yelling, and cursing me for doing this."

"But, I'm not." Sean smiled lightly.

A hot tear cascaded down Katie's cheek, following the scarred paths on her face that Sean was still studying as her cheeks turned red with pain and trickling blood.

"What have you done?" Sean whispered as his thumb gently smoothed over one of her facial scars. His eyes watered while Katie's body trembled.

She choked back her own emotion to answer him. "I have tried...so many times..."

She couldn't get it out. Her molten tears were burning, and her skin was cooking. Her throat was boiling and the bile rising in her throat was burning holes in her esophagus. She hadn't come down off her fiery depression in weeks and it was physically eating her alive.

She couldn't tell him how much she missed him.

She couldn't tell him how much she ached without him.

"I didn't want to see you in the hospital because I knew you would beat yourself up. I knew you would spew 'I'm sorry' more times than you could count, and I figured you had been through enough," Sean admitted.

But all Katie could do was gawk up at him.

"I didn't pick up your phone calls because I thought that talking to me would only serve to hurt you more than you had already hurt yourself. So, I figured some time away from me to cope with a guilt you never needed to feel was the answer."

Katie's eyes danced, wholly and completely shocked between him as her tears carved even deeper crevices into her cheeks.

So much so that white bone began to show when the molten tear dripped off her cheeks and onto the pavement below.

"Does that hurt?" Sean whispered, worried she was causing herself so much pain..

"I thought you hated me," Katie finally uttered. "I thought you really hated me."

"Oh, Katie," Sean breathed before he shook his head. "I could never hate you."

He cupped her burning face with both his hands and dropped his cane before he limped forward one last step. He closed the gap between their two bodies, his lips slanted over hers. She felt the first degrees of her body slowly beginning to settle into place as Sean whispered against her lips, "I love you, Katie."

In that instant, his lips press heavily against hers again, and her fiery facade melted away. Her blaring red hair slipped back into its regular form, and the steaming sack of skin she had dwelled in for weeks pieced itself back together, and the scars on her cheeks filled themselves back in. Her body was healing itself from its own self-inflicted damage, and she wrapped her arms tightly around Sean's neck before breaking the kiss.

"I love you too, Sean," she whispered back.

The two of them stood in the middle of the sidewalk as the heavens above parted, and the rain falling from the sky drenched their bodies in life-giving water as the world passed them both by.

Made in the USA
Monee, IL
11 July 2021